Coffee Cup Tales

Coffee Cup Tales

Stories Inspired by Overheard

Conversations at the Coffee Shop

Richard Keller

Printed in the United States of America
First Printing, 2014
Wooden Pants Publishing

Book design by: Jennifer Schafer
Edited by: Nancy L. Reed

ISBN-13: 978-0-9973535-0-1

DEDICATION

To the baristas, cooks, cashiers, servers, dishwashers, and loud conversationalists around the world that make writers comfortable, creative, and full of carbohydrates and caffeine.

Contents

ACKNOWLEDGMENTS

INTRODUCTION

Swipe   1

Hand Coughing   5

The Eternal Date   25

Saint Bob   29

Coffee and Kismet   49

I Married the Hell Outta Her   63

Wrestlin' for God   65

Dates versus Dating   97

Coffee Prompts   119

ACKNOWLEDGMENTS

It's hard to put together an acknowledgments page when the thanks could take up its own book — one that I'll probably sell as a special edition to this tome. Nevertheless, I'll try to do my best.

Biggest thanks go out to my lovely wife, Awilda. Her encouragement and the porcupine she stuck on my easy chair whenever I wanted to skip writing and watch television motivated me to complete *Coffee Cup Tales*. Hugs and kisses also go out to my children – Samantha, Shannon, Jason, Victoria, and Abigail — for all the times they didn't eat dinner with their father.

The polished stories in this book wouldn't be here without the diligent work of my editor, Nancy L. Reed. I thank her for all the pink comment bubbles she provided with necessary changes, despite the amount of frustrated sighs throughout my revisions.

The cover and interior layout wouldn't have been as beautiful if I didn't have Jennifer Schafer fix them up. Jen, thanks for doing the things I can't do.

I would have never gotten to this point without the Northern Colorado Writers organization, headed first by founder Kerrie Flanagan and now by April Moore. My first NCW conference in 2011 led me to join a critique group, which led me to complete several manuscripts and short stories and eventually gave me the impetus to start Wooden Pants Publishing. Kerrie and April, thank you so much for guiding me and so many other writers on the path to greatness.

There is always a last thank you, and mine goes to the coffee shops and small cafes of Fort Collins, Colorado. Without your flavored doses of caffeine, comfort food, free Internet, and great acoustics to overhear snippets of conversation in the next room, *Coffee Cup Tales* would never have come to fruition.

INTRODUCTION

Creatives have a unique super power, and it has nothing to do with the ability to survive on cheese spray and Red Bull. Rather, it involves the way they see the world. They have the ability to look at an image or catch a snippet of conversation and form a piece of art around it. It doesn't matter if they're working on something else at the time. The moment a new idea worms their way into their heads it has to be put down in some form for future reference.

This is how the stories in *Coffee Cup Tales* were created. A simple sentence, an action, or even a one or two word phrase floated into my brain while I worked on something else. The opening of a new document, a title, and perhaps one or two sentences of story cemented the idea for the future.

In *Coffee Cup Tales* you'll find stories of love, faith, crayons, and hand coughing. I hope you'll laugh, cry, and shout of its greatness in your favorite coffee shop.

"Even bad coffee is better than no coffee at all."
David Lynch

Swipe

"The ticket prices have gone down."

"For what?" inquired Hussain.

"The concert," replied Trisha.

"What concert?"

"The one we texted each other about last week."

Trisha swiped her smartphone's screen to pull up the messaging records.

"See?" She showed Hussain the text.

"I don't even remember that conversation." He pulled up his own records with a swish of his finger. "I remember the text session we had about the airline tickets."

"To Philly?"

Hussain nodded and showed his screen to Trisha.

"Philly is one of the worst airports in America," he said.

"Is it?"

Trisha accessed the smartphone's virtual keyboard with a flick of her manicured index finger and entered the subject of Philadelphia International Airport into its search field.

"Huh, you're right," she confirmed. "Philly is the worst. Let me send you the article."

With a swipe she emailed a copy of the article to Hussain's.

"This is the one *I* sent you last week," he said.

"Really?"

Hussain searched his browser history, selected an entry with a tap, and showed it to Trisha.

"Wow, I'm a ditz," she replied with a slight smile.

The two continued to swipe and type as their coffees got cold and the beeps, pings, and clacks of other customers' portable electronic devices rose and fell inside the cozy and popular coffee bar.

"Looks like rain," Trisha stated.

"Hmm," Hussain responded, still looking at his display.

"Says so in my weather app," Trish clarified, despite the fact the large window they sat in front of was streaked with raindrops.

"Doesn't rain too much anymore around here," Hussain said. "I think it's due to global warming."

"Why do you say that?"

Hussain caressed his screen and displayed an animated info-graphic on global warming that featured a slowly melting baby glacier explaining climate change.

"How adorable. Makes you feel better about our environmental problems," Trisha said.

"Sure. I guess," Hussain replied with a shrug.

Silence enveloped the two. Trisha became engrossed in a YouTube video. Her laughter broke the digital quiet of the shop several times.

Hussain made a final swipe on the tablet and took the last gulp of his now chilly coffee.

"Well, I've gotta go."

"So soon?" Trisha asked with eyes still locked on her phone.

"Yeah, I wasn't even supposed to be here in the first place."

Trisha looked up at Hussain. The switch from LED to natural light enlarged her pupils.

"What do you mean?"

"I broke up with you."

"Did you?"

"I told you over coffee last week," Hussain said. "In fact, right at this very table."

"We met last week?" Trisha selected her calendar app and reviewed her previous appointments. "I don't have anything listed."

"I told you in person. Then I texted, emailed, and left a Skype message. You acknowledged receipt of everything."

Trisha scanned through the histories of all of her apps. "Yeah, I did that. I guess I just acknowledged them out of habit and didn't actually look at them."

"I'm not surprised." Hussain packed up his electronics and put on his coat. "Take care, Trish."

"Wait!"

Hussain looked into Trisha's eyes, now slightly moist with tears. He realized he never really gazed into them during the time they were dating.

"Why did you decide to break up with me?" she asked.

"We don't communicate."

Hussain pushed in his chair and walked out into the rain.

"Black as the devil, hot as hell, pure as an angel, sweet as love."
Charles Maurice de Talleyrand

Hand Coughing

"Someone once said something about love. I can't remember who, probably a guy or a girl, and they placed the word in the middle of sappy stuff even Hallmark considers too syrupy. Anyway, this male or female philosopher or reality star pretty much said love isn't what a person feels. Instead, it's what the other person does."

I waited while my English Literature students absorbed the tirade I unleashed upon them. They all stared at me in various stages of incomprehension due to misunderstanding or massive hangovers.

"Excuse me, Professor?" asked Rita, a student who bugged the hell out of me during the best of days. "How does this relate to Henry Miller?"

"Henry Miller also talked about love. He said the best way to get over a woman is to put them in a piece of literature. Or maybe it was porn. I can't remember which one exactly."

"Professor?" Rita inquired again, "What does *that* have to do with the works of Henry Miller?"

"Not a damn thing," I answered. "What I'm trying to get through to your somewhat flexible brains is you can't get over a person through writing, or song, or setting a flaming bag of crap on their stoop and running away."

The students turned to each other with questioning expressions.

"If you find something wrong with a partner, it's over. It could be the way they eat, or sleep, or praise Justin Bieber songs. It doesn't matter the reason. You find a singular bad trait and the relationship is kaput."

"Did you just break up with someone, Professor?" another student asked.

"What? Me? No, no relationship. Sure, the sex was absolutely inspiring, but once she ate peanut butter out of the jar with a spoon it ended. It didn't even help she did it naked."

The students' reactions were a combination of horror, amazement, and fear I would rampage through the lecture hall.

"Nope, the whole thing ended when the spoon cracked the smooth surface of the peanut butter. It's meant for sandwiches and sometimes cookies, not as an after-coitus snack!"

"Sir?" asked another student, "are we actually going to learn something today?"

"In a minute." I waved him away and began to pace the classroom. "I mean, how does someone end up the love of your life if they don't take peanut butter seriously? They might as well eat a stick of butter. There's no hope, I tell you."

Students began to pack up their laptops and books.

"No. Hope. At. All." I emphasized each word with a clap of my hands.

I looked up to see most of the class headed out the door.

"Go, young ones! Live your lives free of irreverent peanut butter eaters. Stay single and independent."

The last student stopped and turned in the doorway.

"Great class, Professor. You need to do more of these."

"Heck of a performance this morning, Nathaniel."

"Please let me crawl under your desk to die," I requested of Donald Levine, head of the English Department.

"Henry Miller? Peanut butter? Hallmark? Sounds educational, yet esoteric."

"Who told you?"

"Everyone in the class," Donald answered. "Plus a few more who heard you from the hallway."

"Ohh …"

"And I think someone heard you from the parking lot."

"Forget hiding under your desk," I said. "Give me a space beneath the floorboards."

"Nathaniel, you need to get past this. You broke up with Claire almost a month ago."

"I know," I buried my head in my hands.

"You seemed fine. What happened?"

"I saw her at the supermarket … buying peanut butter."

I looked up to see Donald shaking his head and buried my own skull deeper into my palms.

"I think it's time for you to leave, Nathaniel."

"Forever?"

I heard Donald sigh. "Just for today, maybe tomorrow. Let your student assistant take over. Get some rest, read a book, avoid all peanut butter, and come back refreshed."

"I don't know if I ca—."

"You've gone through this before, Nathaniel," Donald said. "Remember Janet?"

"Right. Bed head." I shuddered at the memory.

"Or Narissa?"

"Goat laugh."

"You adjusted after those relationships broke up," Donald said. "You'll recover from this one."

"Okay." I rubbed my face and stood. "And what if I don't?"

"Well," Donald contemplated, "the Psychology Department always needs despondent males for their clinical trials."

Donald smiled, and I left his office feeling more humiliated than I had when I entered.

The time off did me some good. I graded papers, worked on my novel, slept for fifteen hours, sat and cried in a corner of my kitchen, and removed anything from my cupboard with a Jif or Skippy label. Donald firmly suggested I take the time to make sure I purged myself of all past relationship guilt.

Tired of seeing the walls of my apartment, I walked to a nearby coffee shop. I settled into one of the arm chairs, placed a steaming latte on the table, and began to read a new book from one of my favorite authors. It lacked her usual vampires, werewolves, and angst-driven female protagonists, but it still entertained me with its zombies, ghosts, and angst-driven male protagonist.

Cough. Cough.

The sound interrupted my concentration. I looked around to find the culprit but didn't see anyone with cold or allergy symptoms. In a few seconds I returned to the book.

Cough. Cough.

I looked up again, saw no one in particular.

Cough.

I turned around. Behind me, a woman coughed into her palm.

"You're coughing into your hand?" I asked.

"Excuse me?"

"You're hand coughing." I raised my palm to my mouth to imitate what she did.

"Right. Is there a problem with that?"

"In so many ways." I dropped my book on the armrest and turned to face her. "It causes the spread of infection, for example."

"Says who?"

"The CDC, NIH, my mother."

"And your mother is?"

"Um, my mother," I answered.

"Okay, and how are you supposed to cough?"

"Into your elbow."

I brought the crook of my elbow up to my mouth and faked a cough.

"Ah, I see," she said. "Good to know. Thanks."

Cough.

"You did it again," I said.

"Force of habit."

"You should break it. Maybe I can help you over a coffee or perhaps dinner?"

She titled her head and gazed at me.

"Seriously?"

"Sure," I said. "I can't let you spread germs around."

"Hold on," she said, "I need to put this in perspective. You just flirted with me?"

"Yes."

"By criticizing the way I spread disease?"

"I asked if you wanted to have a coffee or dinner," I corrected.

"So, you just asked me out on a date?" she queried.

"Well, yes."

"Oh, for Pete's sake!"

She stood, went out the back door, and sat down in the coffee house's patio area. I snuck a picture of her with my smartphone. Like a secret agent looking at pictures of an enemy's missile facility, I examined her image and fell head-over-heels in like.

"Oh, for Pete's sake!"

"Funny," I said to Donald, "that's exactly what she said before leaving."

"I'm not surprised, Nathaniel, considering what you did ranks in the upper echelons of clinical insanity."

"How do you know about clinical insanity?"

"Friends in the Psychology Department," Donald said. "By the way, they're *very* interested in seeing you."

"For what?" I asked.

Donald tilted his head and gazed at me. "Seriously?"

"She also said that to me," I admitted.

"Nathaniel ..."

"I don't need that kind of help, Donald. I need to find the identity of this woman. I need to meet her again."

"You never saw her before?"

"This is a pretty big college town," I said, pulling on my beard for some comfort. "She may be a visitor, a researcher, or an instructor from another department."

"So how do you expect me to find out who she is?"

"I ... snapped a picture as she left."

"Insanity and stalking. Okay, I'm calling my friend." Donald reached for the phone.

"Can you just take a look at the picture before you commit me?" I pleaded. "You may know her."

"It's a pretty big college town, Nathaniel."

"Just look."

I passed my phone to Donald. He looked at the picture, his eyes widened, and he rubbed his face in frustration.

"Do you know her?"

"I do," Donald responded. "Mostly because ..."

"I still don't know why my father requested I meet you here."

Rachel Levine sat across from me at a table in one of the coffee shop's smaller rooms. She looked even more stunning than when I first saw her.

"Because your father is a lovely fellow," I answered. "Great instructor, terrific boss, and wonderful humanitarian."

Rachel smiled. Animated butterflies and hummingbirds appeared above her.

"Well, you sure know how to butter up a person."

The mention of butter reminded me of eating a stick of butter, which reminded me of peanut butter, which reminded me of my last failed relationships. I pushed the memories aside and pressed ahead.

"Look, I have to apologize for being a bit out of line."

"A bit?" Her eyebrows arched at my statement.

"Okay, grossly out of line. I wasn't in the best shape, and I shouldn't have said what I did."

"Well, my father explained your situation to me, and I can certainly understand where you're coming from." Rachel leaned in closer. "I mean, who in their right mind eats peanut butter from the jar?"

A chorus of angels sang in my head.

"Exactly. I just thought we could get to know each other a little better. See if this could go somewhere."

"Like where?" Rachel asked.

Marriage, children, a house on the lake, my inner voice proclaimed.

"Maybe a first date?" My outer voice asked.

"This isn't the first date?"

"Let's call it the pre-qualifier," I corrected.

"Okay, what do you want to know?"

"Well," I sat straighter in my chair, "you can start by telling me what you're doing at the college."

"That's a funny story. You see …"

Cough. Cough.

Her hand went to her mouth. The world darkened around me.

"… and they were short a faculty member, so the department head hired me to teach a course on why Jar Jar Binks is one of the classic characters in cinema."

The darkness cleared, and I chuckled at the story despite not hearing the first part of it.

"You're right, that is funny."

The statement sounded forced in my head.

"How did you get into films?"

Cough. Cough.

Again, light faded around me. I saw her lips move but didn't hear her say anything.

"… though no one understands why I think *Bachelor Party* should have won the *Palm d' or* at the Cannes Film Festival back in the 1980s."

"Oh, I agree," I said once the scene brightened again.

Cough. Cough.

"I'm sorry," I said with a smile, "but you're doing it again."

"Doing what?"

"Coughing into your hand."

She examined her appendage as if she just now realized its existence.

"I've coughed into my hand all my life," she admitted. "As far as I know, I haven't spread a plague to anyone."

Cough. Cough.

"There you go again," I protested.

"Did I?" An evil smirk stretched across her features.

Cough. Cough.

"Stop."

Cough. Cough. Cough.

"Please stop."

Rachel took a deep breath and put her hand right to her mouth. *COUGH.*

"Dammit! Please stop the friggin hand coughing!"

Everyone turned to look at me. Even those listening to something loud on their earbuds popped them out.

"A musical," I said, rubbing my beard. "We're rehearsing a musical called *Hand Coughing.*"

The patrons and employees continued to stare, and I felt heat build in my face.

"It's a new Stephen Sondheim piece. We're going through one of the climactic scenes."

Rachel confounded look matched the rest of the customers.

"Don't worry, we'll move the dance number outside."

Normal conversation slowly resumed, but Rachel continued to stare.

"Um …," I started.

"You know, for some reason I like you. I barely know you, and you may have psychotic tendencies, but I like you."

She stood and placed her coughing hand on my own.

"Call me after you get yourself fixed up."

Rachel walked out the door.

I grabbed a napkin, wiped my hand, then slammed my head down on the table several times in frustration.

"Hey," someone from the next table leaned over, "is this the scene in the musical where the heroine gets up and leaves?"

"I'm nuts."

My students stilled, fingers poised over their laptop keyboards.

"Professor, who said that?" asked Rita.

"I'm sure plenty of people," I answered. "The publisher who picked up *Fifty Shades of Grey* comes to mind. This time I'm talking about myself."

The class closed their laptops.

"She's attractive, smart, and knows her film history, yet I can't get past the point she coughs into her hand."

"Excuse me?" asked another student.

I gave them an example of a hand cough.

"Aren't you supposed to cough into your elbow?" another student inquired.

"Exactly." I pointed to the student for emphasis. "Problem is, I can't get beyond the minor, idiotic, totally disgusting trait which could cause a potential zombie outbreak."

My students regarded me like the patrons of the coffee shop.

"Okay, I'm exaggerating about the zombies, but I still don't understand why I do it all the time."

"You're not ready to love."

I looked at Rita, who made the statement. She didn't crawl under her desk or lean back in her chair to avoid my reach. She looked me directly in the eyes.

"Everybody, leave," I said.

I pointed at Rita.

"Except you."

The rest of the class shoved their way out of the door in record time. Rita began to gather her belongings.

"What did you mean by that?"

"I've taken two of your classes so far, Professor, and each one was punctuated by one of your failed relationships. We've heard you rant and rave about how she didn't live up to your standards or she wiped her mouth with her sleeve."

"Lord, that's worse than hand coughing." I shivered at the images forming in my mind.

"Thing is, we don't hear how you screwed everything up."

I looked at Rita, thoughts of the many ways I could make the rest of the semester miserable ran through my head.

"You have these preconceived perceptions about love and attraction. Maybe it's from all the books and poetry you read, or maybe it came from the way your parents acted. Hell, you could've gotten your understanding of love from *Maxim* for all I know. Whatever way, it's blocked you from realizing what true affection should be."

"You're twenty-one or twenty-two, right?" I asked sharply. "What do you know about love and relationships?"

"You're thirty or thirty-five, right?" Rita returned calmly. "Shouldn't you know more about love and relationships?"

A tense quiet hung over us as our barbs sank in.

"*Touché*," I conceded.

"Do you think everything perfectly matches up when you're in a relationship?" she asked. "God, how boring. I've been dating this guy who reads the newspaper in the nude each morning. Granted, he has a smokin' body and, well, you know ..."

"Can we get to the point?"

"I was about to," she said with a smile.

"Rita ..."

"Despite his idiosyncrasies, I enjoy spending time with him."

"Do you love him?"

"Jury's still out on that, Professor, but I know I won't leave him because he reads up on current events sans clothing. It'll be due to the fact I'm not interested in him anymore.

Rita closed her backpack, slung it over her shoulder, and approached me.

"Professor ... Nathaniel, you're a great instructor, and I intend to take another class of yours before I graduate. It's mostly because you keep me interested, but also because I have a small crush on you."

I opened my mouth to respond, but Rita held up her hand to stop me.

"I'm also crushing on David Beckham, so don't be too flattered. You're my favorite when you're on your A game, not when you're moping about peanut butter and hand coughing. Get inside yourself and figure it all out before it's too late.

She caressed my beard and headed out the door.

"You know, you're still a pain in my side," I called out to her.

"I know." Rita closed the classroom door behind her with a quiet snap.

"The purpose of a class is to have the students *remain* in the room."

I sat rigid in one of Donald's office chairs. He stood over me with a look of mingled annoyance and sympathy.

"I was totally out of line," I confessed.

"And flirting with a student, no less."

"What?"

"Someone saw you chatting up a female student."

"It was Rita," I said.

"Oh." Donald's face softened. "You hate her."

"I think she's a pain, but I don't hate her. Anyway, the only thing that happened was a harsh berating of my actions."

"Well, someone had to do it," Donald said.

"Lord, I'm nuts." I lifted my face to the ceiling to see if I could find an answer in the water stains.

"You're not nuts, but you're starting to catch the attention of some of the higher-ups."

My attention snapped back to Donald, who now sat down behind his desk and folded his hands on top.

"One of the Vice Deans visited me today. A few students and a couple of parents addressed concerns about your teaching abilities."

"Are you kidding me?"

"And some of those parents happen to be, um, important donors to the college."

"Crap," I said.

"I would've used a more colloquial term, since I am the head of the English Department, but your simple epithet works."

I sighed and raised my hands in surrender.

"I need help," I admitted.

"No kidding," Donald said and passed a slip of paper across the desk. "I called ahead to the Psychology Department. My friend is waiting for you to visit."

"So, do you have romantic feelings toward your mother?" asked Janice Tupelo.

"Excuse me?" I responded.

"Sorry, it's a department joke. You know, Oedipus and—"

"I'm aware," I said in a monotone.

"Right, English professor. I forgot."

I kept my focus on Janice, even though I wanted to roll my

eyes at her. Or make a break for it and run screaming down the hall. Unfortunately, the smallness of the room would've easily allowed her to block my exit.

"Tell me what's going on," Janice coerced.

"I would've thought Donald told you all about it."

"He did," Janice confirmed. "I just want to hear it from the source."

"Well, I'm messed up," I started.

"That's what they all say."

"All who?"

"Everyone who comes to see me," Janice said. "In the end, none of them are messed up."

Silence.

"Well, some of them are. This one gal —"

"I can't maintain a relationship," I said to break through her meandering thoughts. "No matter how great things are going, I always find the one stupid thing that ends it all."

"Like Seinfeld."

"Huh?"

"Jerry, on *Seinfeld*," Janice answered. "In every episode there's this one thing Jerry second-guesses in his relationship, regardless how attractive and personable they are."

"You're comparing my real idiosyncrasies to those of a television character?"

Janice leaned in closer.

"Aren't we all characters in a giant television series filmed in front of an audience of Earth's citizens and watched by God?"

More silence.

"Is there anyone else out there," I pointed beyond the office door, "who can help me?"

"Sorry, they all went home for the day," Janice said. "You're stuck with me."

"Swell."

"Why did you say that?"

"What?"

"Swell," she answered. "Why did you say it so sarcastically?"

I replayed the moment.

"Well, I—"

"Is there something you don't like about me?"

I attempted to put together an answer in my head, but nothing seemed to work.

"Perhaps you find something annoying about me."

I closed my eyes to avoid her now-piercing gaze.

"Go ahead, you can say it," she egged on. "You won't hurt my feelings."

"You don't act like a real therapist," I blurted out. "Your jokes suck, you wander into your own memories, and you equate problems to those of fictional characters."

"Am I good looking?" she asked.

"Absolutely." I couldn't stop it from coming out.

"But my actions make me a pain in the ass, correct?"

"They sure do."

Janice stared, and I stewed. Something akin to comprehension clicked in my brain, and I gasped in awareness.

"Damn," I whispered. "I did it to you."

"Yep," Janice confirmed. "And it hurt my feelings."

"I'm sorry."

"Just kidding," she said with a smile. "Trust me, I've heard worse. In fact, some of what the Dean of Students said to me would curl your ear hairs."

I brushed my hands against my ears.

"So, let's settle a few things," Janice said. "One, you're not insane, unless you see annoying things in imaginary people."

I shook my head.

"Two, you do have issues that need further examination."

"Okay, what's next?" I asked.

She tapped her lips with an index finger, then nodded at an internal decision.

"Time to visit your past," she said. "Come back in a week and we'll discuss."

The next days were uncomfortable. I managed to teach classes without any further emotional tirades but got distracted by visits from Donald and other college administrators. They tried to observe unobtrusively from the back rows of the classroom. Still, their presence ratcheted up my already tense nerves.

Then there was Rachel. I called her several times to explain myself. In return I got voice mail or an occasional "Call me when you figure it out" followed by an abrupt disconnect. I tried to ask Donald about what Rachel thought of me. He provided an even terser "Figure it out" before he kicked me out of his office.

I became so anxious I almost broke down Janice's office door in order to start the appointment on time.

"So, how's it going?" she asked pleasantly.

"Terrible," I answered, raising a shaky hand to wipe sweat from my forehead.

"Why?"

"Everywhere I go I mentally criticize those nearby. Colleagues, students, people who walk down the hallway or sit at tables in the coffee shop. I can't stop myself."

"It overwhelms you."

"My God, yes," I said.

"Good. We're making progress," Janice said.

My mouth opened in shock.

"Come again?" I asked.

"You're on your way to recovery," Janice confirmed.

"Care to explain?"

"No."

My mouth opened again.

"I'm kidding," she said. "Jokester, remember?"

I surveyed her, lips sore from biting down on them.

"You never knew you had an issue before this," Janice answered. "You thought everyone else was screwed up. Now you understand the opposite, so what was normal now seems odd and, I'm guessing, uncomfortable."

"Nauseatingly uncomfortable," I corrected.

"That's natural," Janice said. "Think of someone who stops drinking or smoking. They feel their habits are fine. A few days or weeks after they give it up they see things in others who smoke or drink that they never realized. It can be jarring."

"How do I fix it?"

"We talk about your mother."

Janice grabbed a file folder from her desk.

"From what you wrote in your profile, you were an only child."

I nodded.

"And your father died while you were still a toddler."

"Yes."

"Tell me about your relationship with your mom."

"Wonderful," I said. "Sure, a little overprotective sometimes. People call it helicopter parenting these days. Still, she was smart and provided me with great advice I still carry to this day."

"Like what?" Janice asked.

"The information on hand coughing, for instance."

"Right, that started all of this."

"How did you know?"

"I spoke to Donald, remember?" she answered. "Need to get background on my patients, just in case they're reluctant to talk."

"It's a scientifically-proven fact," I said.

"I'm not saying it isn't," Janice said. "Did your mother get defensive when someone tried to deflate her arguments?"

"I'm not defensive," I said loudly.

She grinned at me.

"Um, well, she did get somewhat argumentative," I said, my head down to hide the dark shade of red it had become.

"And did she do it a lot?"

"Sometimes. She wasn't really a social person."

Janice kept silent.

"People tended to fall into behavioral patterns and exhibit certain traits my mother didn't want to deal with."

"For example?"

"Well, most of the people where she worked had one fault or another, like they were selfish or greedy or just tended to hang out with the wrong crowd."

"Uh-huh."

"And she didn't really get along with her family. She said her brother drank too much, her father cheated, and her mother wasn't very bright."

"Right."

"And I didn't have many close friends in school. My mother seemed … to find something wrong … with them or their parents, and …"

I stopped and examined an invisible point on the wall behind Janice. Memories of my childhood flooded back in a movie-like montage, displaying examples of what I just explained.

I looked back at Janice, who smiled at me with genuine warmth.

"There you go," she said gently. "Now we can work on the healing."

"I should kill my father for giving you my home address."

I passed the bouquet of roses to Rachel.

"They're not full of poison, are they? Or something to paralyze my hands?"

"May I come in?" I asked.

"Any weapons on you? Perhaps hand sanitizer?"

"No? Why?"

"You may need them if you get me pissed off again," Rachel invited me in.

"I need to apologize." I found a seat on the couch.

"Good start," Rachel said. "And promising. Never had a relationship where the man apologized for his actions so much."

"I've been a total jackass."

"More good news," she said. "Keep going."

"Hey, I spent hours memorizing this," I admitted. "Can you let me do it right?"

Rachel smiled and nodded for me to continue.

"I'm not just apologizing to you. I'm apologizing to everyone I broke up with because of my idiocy. See, a pain in the ass student of mine told me I don't know how to love, and a quirky therapist helped me understand why."

"I like them both," she said.

"So do I, but don't let them know. After I decided not to report either of them, I determined they were absolutely right. When I met someone and began noticing their, um ..."

"Totally disgusting and unfathomable habits?" Rachel answered for me.

"Let's go with that," I agreed. "When I began noticing those traits, my mind went to a scenario where I spent the next fifty years watching you cough into your hand or finding an empty peanut butter jar with a spoon inside. But I shouldn't have done that."

"No kidding."

"I should've pushed those thoughts aside and focused more on the happy times we could have. Unfortunately, I became so obsessed with the traits, I got ..."

"Distracted? Crazed? Looney Tunes?"

"Right, though my therapist puts it in more clinical terms."

Rachel put down the flowers and sat next to me.

"So, Nathaniel, what are you saying?"

"I'm saying I'd like to try this again," I answered. "And no matter how many times you cough into your hand, I'll look past it and focus on how I like you and would be interested in developing a relationship."

"And avoiding the wrath of my father should you mess this up?"

"It crossed my mind."

Rachel chuckled, then kissed me on my cheek. It felt warm and comforting.

"Sure, what the hell," she said. "And, by the way, you got it right."

"What?"

"Coughing into your elbow. I did some research online and found it's much more hygienic."

"So, you'll consider coughing into your elbow from now on?" I asked.

"Heck, no."

I smiled and grasped her hands. "That's fine, actually."

"Henry Miller once said the best way to get over a woman is to put them in a piece of literature."

I heard groans and saw eye-rolls from my students.

"But he was wrong."

The groans and eye-rolling stopped.

"No one way helps you to get over a love or an intense like. People get past their broken relationships in any way they can to avoid the pain and emptiness it produces. Sometimes it means revisiting a past you once believed normal. Other times it means becoming slightly obsessive and insane. Mostly, it means getting over yourself."

The room grew quiet, everyone's attention on me. In the front row, I saw Rita smile.

"Here's the thing, kids. Don't let authors or directors or real housewives tell you how to get over a relationship or get through one. Quash your idiotic obsessions, and leave it up to your instincts and the love and affection boiling inside you to make the best determination on how to proceed. In the end you may surprise yourself at how well you recover.

"Oh, and don't worry about the little things. If you truly enjoy a person for whom they are, their idiosyncrasies won't matter a damn in the end. In fact, they may become more endearing in time."

"Who wrote that, Professor?" one of the students broke the silence with the question.

"No one. It actually came from someone fairly wise for her youngish age."

Rita blushed.

My phoned buzzed, and I glanced at the text message displayed.

"Had a great time last night. Let's do it again tonight. I'll bring tissues. Rachel."

I smiled, put the phone away, and looked back at my class.

"Okay, open your laptops and tablets, and let's see what else Henry Miller had to say."

The Eternal Date

"… and that's why I lived in my BMW for a few months."

"Interesting." *I can't feign this enthusiasm much longer.*

"Well, dealing with the wolves and the muggers was the most interesting part," Antonio chuckles and sips his latte.

I'm looking down at my coffee cup with the little slit you drink out of so you don't get burnt and sue the place. I continue to wear my heavy winter coat, despite sitting at a table that butts up to the fireplace grate.

Antonio seems oblivious to it all.

In fact, the only thing he seems interested in is my eyes. He doesn't lose contact with them, not even when he slurps his coffee like a dog coming out of the desert heat in desperate need of water. I find the constant eye contact creepy and the sound of his liquid consumption loud in my ears.

All in all, not the greatest date.

"You're very pretty, Mandy."

"Thanks."

A smile isn't going to happen. He's going to need to settle for a tight-lipped grimace.

"I'm glad you agreed to a second date."

"Thanks."

Does he realize I'm repeating myself?

I can't believe I'm on another date with Antonio. Yeah, he seemed attractive enough the first time he stepped up to the café's counter and placed his order. Maybe it was the heat of the kitchen or the fact I just completed a double-shift that prompted me to say Yes.

I guess the first date went sort of okay. I laughed a few times at the start, then things got weird. Well, he got weird. I kept my mouth shut and nodded at all his stories about the famous people he knew, his trips around the world, the freelance mercenary work he did in Afghanistan and Syria, the fortune he accumulated during a crazy session of Texas Hold Em' at Caesar's. It felt like bluster with a hint of BS thrown in for flavor.

He tried to kiss me on the cheek at the end of our first date. I gave him a firm handshake and "See ya" instead. I thought he would get the idea another date was out of the question and delete my phone number, email, Skype handle, and IM nickname from all his electronic devices.

I still don't know how he got all of my personal information.

Heck, I wiped the evening out of my memory once I got home. Except for Antonio's eyes – they haunted me. Every time I closed my own that night I saw his in my mind. Irises golden brown like a glass of bourbon, pupils orange-red with flame.

He comes into the cafe again a few days later, orders the same thing, and asks me to go out again. I want to throw a soda in his face and use various colorful and filthy words to tell him to leave. Out of the blue I say Yes.

He smiles, takes his order, and departs. My head feels foggy until he leaves, and I shake it clear to help the next customer. That night his fiery eyes return to my dreams.

Now here I am, coffee cooling in its paper cup, my jacket buttoned all the way to the neck, one foot poised for a quick getaway.

"I think it's time I go." I prepare to depart.

"Why? The night's just begun." The yellow light of the antique ceiling lamp reflects off the enamel of Antonio's teeth.

"I've got an early shift tomorrow and—"

Wait, what is that tingle on my hand? Holy crap, Antonio's holding it! How did I not feel him touch me?

"I think we have a great future together, my Mandy."

I'm not his Mandy. Why can't I open my mouth to scream that at him? And now he's caressing my hand with his thumb. Up and down, slow motion. It's hypnotic.

"You want to be with me, don't you?"

His voice seems far away, like he's in another room or perhaps a cave deep below the cafe's floor. I try to pull away my hand. It's frozen under Antonio's and it won't move.

Soldered may be the better term, because my hand feels hot beneath his.

The burn is rising up my arm. It feels unpleasant.

Why can't I pull my hand free?

"I want you to join me in my journeys, Mandy. Above and below the surface of the Earth."

Below? What the hell does he mean by below?

My eyes are wide now, and my heart beats a rapid cadence in my throat. No one sitting at the other tables seems to notice what's going on with us. Not even that guy complaining about the way his partner is coughing into her hand.

Actually, now that I look closely at the other people, they're barely moving.

The heat of Antonio's hand reaches my shoulder and is now making a fast trek across my collarbone. I'm also feeling an increased warmth on my cheeks.

The fire. Is the fire bigger than when we first got here? I don't remember anyone coming in to stoke the flames.

"I haven't had a queen in a while, and it does get lonely where I rule."

Rule? Wasn't he telling me about living in a car and fighting off wolves? My God, that was the lie! I think, no, I know he's telling the truth. He wants to take me away and be some sort of consort. Why can't I yell in horror at the top of my lungs?

He increases his caress on my hand, and the fire grows bigger. It's past the grate and licking the brickwork. I see reflections of the flames in the pictures on the opposite wall and the windows that look out onto the street.

Why isn't anyone around here calling the fire department or running for an extinguisher?

"Are you ready, Mandy?"

Something is pulling my gaze toward Antonio's eyes. He's still staring at me, and his pupils reflect the flames.

Hold on, not reflect — the fire is burning in them!

It's what I saw in my dreams and found unbelievable. Now I'm finding it intriguing, sensual.

Why am I so aroused by this?

"Time to take you away from this boring life."

Boring? I have friends, family, a steady job, a nice apartment. Then again, I rarely speak to my friends and family, my apartment's too small, and I'm on a career path taking me nowhere. I have a chance to do something with myself.

Wait. Why am I thinking this?

"Time to start the adventure of your lifetime."

The flames now reach the ceiling and are the width of the fireplace itself. But the mirror on the top of the mantle doesn't reflect any of it.

I'm not ready for this. "I'm ready." *Where the hell did that come from?*

I'm up now, and the tables and their patrons are gone from the room. Antonio still holds my hand, and I feel pleasure encompass my entire body. Now I hear a roar.

There's an opening within the flame.

"Let's go, my precious Queen."

I go into the flame. It doesn't feel hot, and my skin isn't burning. How …

Saint Bob

"Every time someone comes up to me and asks how I became a saint, I always answer with 'Practice, practice, practice.'"

"Uh-huh."

I snort at my therapist's response to the statement. She's like all the others who've heard it—they never laugh. Probably due to the fact they're too young to remember the original joke about getting to Carnegie Hall.. Of course, it could be old as time itself. Heck, people could've said the same thing when someone asked how they got to the Globe Theatre or the Coliseum.

"You see, Jack Benny said it when he—"

"I know the joke, Bob," says Dr. Cosmas.

"Saint Bob," I correct.

"Excuse me?"

"I call myself Saint Bob. Saint Robert seems too formal."

"Okay."

Cosmas is not my original therapist. She's the eighth in a series of psychological engineers I've encountered since my enlightenment. For some reason, the others kept dropping me once I insisted on my living sainthood.

"Do you perform miracles?" she asks.

"Well, I don't perform them yet, but I'm pretty sure I will at some point in time."

"Were you always a manifestation of God's will?"

"Nope," I answer. "I worked in IT for fifteen years. Pretty mundane tasks—installing computers, troubleshooting, asking customers if they plugged USB adapters into their tablets to use their wireless keyboards."

"Sure," says Cosmas. "So, when did the transformations take place?"

"I slammed my head into the bottom of a desk while hooking up a new computer. Blacked out for a few minutes and had a huge bump on my head. I called it Little Bob."

Cosmas looks up from her note-taking.

"Are you serious?"

"Nah. Just wanted to make sure you were paying attention."

"Uh-huh."

"Well, not long after, I began to have weird dreams. I mean, weirder than ones I had about flying or going to an install in my underwear. Thing is, I dreamed the same scenario each night. I finally realized they weren't dreams at all."

"They were visions," Cosmas says.

"How did you know?" I say, eyebrows lifted in curiosity.

"Wild guess," Cosmas answers. "Tell me about them."

"They were filled with smoke, fire, and ear-piercing screams. I could smell the aromas of burning wood and charred meat, and I felt the heat of the flames. I tasted the smoke billowing across the sky. The scariest thing was I couldn't bring myself out of the visions during their progression."

"Did they stop?"

"No," I say. "They changed."

Cosmas' eyebrows lift with curiosity.

"These days I see myself in front of the flames, holding my hands up high and head pointed toward the sky. Each time I just stand there, hot and disintegrating chaos all around me."

"Seems dramatic."

"I wake up drenched in sweat each time."

"Have you been to a doctor?"

"Other than you?" I ask.

"There are plenty of different doctors," she answers.

"Sure. They took X-rays, EEGs, MRIs, and all those other acronym-based tests I couldn't afford."

"And what did they find?"

"Nothing," I answer.

"Excuse me?"

"No blood clots, no tumors, no little men running around checking all the synapses. Everything was clean."

"Huh," Cosmas grunts.

"Excuse me?"

"The manifestation of visions is normally connected with a disruption inside the brain."

"It's not a brain misfire," I say. "God wants me to do something on Earth."

"Has he specifically designated you a living saint?" she asks.

"We don't talk. He just sends me his messages in the form of visions."

"But you don't know what the visions mean."

I shrug.

"Well, I think we need to investigate this further."

I start to get out of my chair, but stop midway.

"Wait, you want me to come back?" I ask.

She nods.

"You're not going to send me to another one of your colleagues? Or to another hospital?"

"Why would I want to do that?" Cosmas asks.

"Because, well, you don't believe me," I answer.

She looks at me for a second, puts her pad and pen down, and leans forward. "When did I ever say I didn't believe you?"

"When –"

I pause and replay the past hour of discussion in my head.

"I don't think you ever said you didn't believe me."

"Something's happening, Saint Bob," she says. "Call it mental or spiritual, I'm here to help you through it."

"Why?"

"It's my job," Cosmas answers, "and I'm damn good at it."

"Cosmas doesn't know what she's talking about."

My friend Edie takes a bite from her scone and chews slowly while I take in her comment.

"At least she didn't kick me out of her office," I respond.

"Probably needs the clients," Edie answers. "Really, you need to go to the hospital and get yourself checked out."

I sigh and regard the coffee shop. Despite how busy it is, we manage to snag a table in the big room with the fireplace. People study, read, converse, and go about their routine lives. Meanwhile, the person in *my* life doubts everything I say.

"Again, they didn't find anything wrong," I state for the hundredth time.

"Then go to another one."

"And you'll pay for all the tests?" I ask.

"I don't have that type of money," Edie says.

"Neither do I."

"Because you quit your job," Edie says.

"Why do I need to work eight hours inside a windowless room when I'm a saint?"

"You're not a saint!"

"Why?"

"Because you're not dead!"

"Who says you need to be deceased to become a saint?" I ask.

"The Bible, the Pope, Catholic doctrine."

"Times change," I counter. "There's a new Pope. Maybe all you need now is a serious injury in order to qualify."

"You bumped your head, Bob. You didn't get crushed by an oncoming train or nailed to a cross."

"Then I would be dead, wouldn't I."

"And we wouldn't be having this stupid conversation," Edie says.

"Actually, I find these debates exhilarating," I state.

"Why do I remain friends with you?" she asks.

"Now that's a question God needs to answer."

Edie curses under her breath and returns to reading the latest copy of *Star* magazine. I smile at my small victory.

"The vision changed last night."

"Totally different than your other ones?" Cosmas asks.

I smile at her use of the word visions to describe what I see. The other therapists practically forced me to say dreams to describe what I saw each night.

"Not too much difference," I say. "Things were still burning around me, and I continued to stand there examining the sky. But this time around I heard something else?"

I pause, and she nods for me to continue.

"A roar, like thunder," I say.

"A thunderstorm?"

"I didn't see any lightning," I say. "It sounded more like a powerful rush of wind."

"A tornado?"

I shake my head. "I don't remember seeing any type of funnel cloud."

She scribbles something into her notepad. Even though I remain her client I wonder if the note says something like "Nuts?"

"Let's go back to the fire," Cosmas instructs. "Why do you think it plays such a prominent role in these visions?"

"Don't know."

"Do you have a fear of fire?"

"I don't think so."

"Any traumatic instances involving fire in your childhood?"

"Not so much as a campfire," I say.

"Have any dreams about fire before?"

"You mean visions?"

She shakes her head.

"Before you hit your head."

"Oh." I clear thoughts of finding another therapist out of my mind. "I don't think so."

She sits straighter in her chair. "Do you recall any dreams prior to hitting your head?"

I'm about to answer but pause with my mouth halfway open. I close my eyes and try to think back to my pre-saint days.

"Come to think of it, no, I don't."

"You told me in our first session about dreams you had of flying or installations in your underwear," Cosmas says.

"Really? Maybe I gave those as examples of standard dreams."

"You mean you really didn't have those dreams before the accident?"

"I honestly couldn't tell you," I answer.

"Interesting."

"Is interesting good or bad?" I ask.

Cosmas scribbles something new in her notes, pauses, and pulls out a prescription pad.

"I'm going to prescribe a mild sedative to see if it makes you sleep better. Perhaps diminish the visions."

"But I don't want them to diminish."

"Excuse me?"

"The visions mean something, Dr. Cosmas," I say. "I've never been a religious person, so I'm not sure if they're telling me about an apocalypse or something less dire."

"I'm pretty sure everything is less dire than the end of the world," she says.

"Regardless, ever since I became a saint, I've known the visions are calling me to do something."

"And that is?"

"Damn if I know."

"I wasn't aware saints could swear."

"Living saint. New rules."

"Well, I'll give you the prescription," Cosmas says. "It's up to you whether you want to fill it."

"Sure."

"Time's up." She stands and heads back to her desk. "However, one more thing."

I give her an anticipatory glance.

"Go out and do something nice for someone."

"Hey, it's Saint Bobbo!"

A chuckle winds its way through the crowd of bar patrons. Charlie, the man who shouts the words, sits at the scratched and chipped bar. It's 11 a.m., which means he's drunk.

"Saint Bobby, come to try your hand at saving me again?"

I smile and sit next to him. The bartender starts to head my way, and I raise my hand to halt him.

"I'll do what I can, Charlie," I say.

"Should've been here an hour ago when I was only buzzed," Charlie says. "Maybe I would've given a crap back then."

Charlie and I used to work together as IT grunts, and he drank back then. It got worse after he got laid off. He lost his house, his family left him, and he ended up living in a dingy and tiny room at the Y. Now, he does menial jobs in order to spend most of his waking and semi-conscious hours on his favorite bar stool.

"How many is he in?" I ask Denny, the bar's owner.

"Several," he says with a scowl. Denny doesn't like me coming to his establishment. He fears he'll go out of business if I cure all the alcoholics sitting in the dark and smoky room.

"You didn't stop him?"

"Why should I?" he answers. "He's a big boy. He should know when to stop."

"You tell 'em, Donny," says Charlie with a heavy slur. "Give me anudder while you're at it."

"Don't do it, Denny," I say, moving toward him.

"What'cha gonna do, saint man? Smite me?"

"Saints don't smite anyone," I answer.

"Good. Then mind your own friggin business."

Denny pours two shots of cheap whiskey and slides them across the bar toward Charlie. He knocks them back in ten seconds.

"Ah, liquid courage," he coos, then slams down one of the glasses to signal for another two shots.

"I think you reached your limit," I say.

"I think you should mind your own goddamn business," Charlie says. "And, by the way, why are you so friggin concerned about me? We barely even talked when we worked together."

"I'm a saint," I say. "It's my job to make sure you're safe."

"Yeah, right."

"Plus, my therapist told me to do something nice today."

"Then save a cat from a tree," Charlie says.

"I'd rather help you," I counter.

"Yeah, well, plenty of drunks in the city. Why don't you go to them?"

"Something just led me to you."

"Wish it would lead you somewhere else, you nutbag."

Denny slides another shot glass down the bar's surface. I halt it with my hand, and its contents spill over the rim of the glass.

"Dammit, that stuff ain't cheap," growls Denny. "Charlie, you're paying for it even though your idiot friend spilled it."

"Yeah, yeah," Charlie mumbles and pulls out a pack of cigarettes. He fumbles one into his mouth, pulls out a lighter, and ignites the tip. Taking a deep inhalation of carcinogens, Charlie removes it from his mouth and lays the lit portion near the edge of the spilled alcohol.

"No!"

I reach for him, and my mind explodes.

I'm in the midst of my fire vision. Things still burn around me, screams are still heard, and the roar I noticed the night before is intensified. I watch myself, and this time I'm able to draw closer. I get a profile image of my vision self and see it crying and pleading for assistance.

The roar increases. I scan upward and see white cracks in the dark sky. There's an intense gust of wind pushing my vision-self forward. I smell fresh air and—

I return to the present, just at the point I lunge for Charlie's arm. I push him off the stool as his cigarette ignites the alcohol spill and creates a flame that speeds down the bar top. The morning drunks notice the fire and become somewhat sober when fear and adrenaline pulse through their bloodstreams. They stumble out the door. Denny grabs a fire extinguisher from under the bar and sprays down its surface, but not before the automatic sprinklers activate and douse the entire room in cold spray.

"Holy Jesus!"

I glance down and see Charlie sitting upright, looking at his cigarette like it were a gun. His expression makes me think some of the drunkenness is now scared out of him.

"So, do you want to try to get some help?"

"I—," he starts.

I stretch my hand down to him. He looks at it, hands me the cigarette, and stands up.

"Sure. What the hell. Can't afford to burn down any more bars, can I."

"There's your miracle, Bob."

"Edie, you know it doesn't work like that."

We don't have the normal coffee shop conversation. Instead, she's now confident I have fulfilled my spiritual assignment.

"Come on, you saved Charlie's life."

"Sure, by human means. It's not like I turned the whiskey into water or anything like that."

"Maybe you did."

"Then it wouldn't have caught fire."

"Well, you have a point there," Edie concedes.

"There's something else."

"Hmm?"

"I had a vision just before the event happened."

Edie stays silent for a few seconds, her gaze never wavers from my face.

"I'm driving you to the hospital."

"Again with this? I told you the doctors said—"

"Obviously, the doctors don't know crap." There's no longer mild frustration in Edie's voice. Now it's pure anger. "I could understand having these dreams—"

"Visions," I correct.

"—these *dreams* at night or when you're napping, but not while you're wide awake. That's not right."

"Maybe it's a sign," I say.

"A sign of what?"

"That the miracle involves a fire bigger than a simple alcohol-induced one started by a drunk."

She snorts at me with derision.

"You're sick, Bob. Not a saint, not a messenger from above, not someone able to conduct a miracle anytime soon. Just sick."

She reaches over the table and pokes her finger into my forehead.

"There's something going on in there that's making you believe these things."

"Well, if that's the case, poking me in the head probably isn't helping."

She pauses in mid-poke, then smiles and sits back down.

"Edie, I appreciate the concern. Trust me, if I felt something off with my mental state, I'd ask you to throw me in the nearest ambulance. I'm facing something different than a tumor or an aneurysm. I'm about to do something, well, amazing."

Edie raises her hands in front of her in a sign of defeat.

"All right, you win – for now. I won't strap you down to your chair and force you to go get your head checked again."

"Such a kind friend," I say and squeeze her shoulder.

"Yeah, yeah."

She becomes silent and focuses on a small puddle of coffee that drips onto the tabletop. For a few seconds I'm sad for her. She doesn't comprehend what I feel right now. I don't think she ever will.

"So, what're you going to do?"

"Something I should have done at the start of the visions," I answer. "Talk to someone who regularly speaks to God."

"I'm not too sure what you're telling me, Bob."

I scrutinize Father Ephrem's face. He doesn't display anger or disbelief. His expression indicates an inability to digest the new information I present to him.

"I need help to find out what miracle I'm supposed to perform."

"As a saint," he says.

"Yes."

"A living saint."

"Yes."

"A living saint who has visions at all hours of the day."

"Well, just the late morning and nighttime right now," I correct.

"Right. My apologies."

Father Ephrem looks down to the Formica countertop of his Rescue Café, then he turns and tends to a half-dozen burgers sizzling on a nearby griddle. I enjoy spending time at the cafe watching how he serves up burgers and fries to the destitute who come in during lunch.

"There's no such thing as a living saint," he says when he returns to the counter.

"So I'm told on a constant basis."

"I mean, lots of folks performed miracles while alive—Mother Teresa, for example. However, they aren't revealed until they die and are up for sainthood."

"Didn't Jesus do the same thing?"

Father Ephrem opens his mouth to respond, shuts it, and turns to empty the deep fryer.

"He's the son of God, Bob," he calls back over his shoulder.

"Isn't he the Son, the Father, and the Holy Ghost?"

"We're still working that out." Father Ephrem sprinkles salt on the fries. "What I'm trying to explain is he wasn't just a normal man."

"But he lived among the common folks, didn't he?"

"Bob, you're confusing things here."

"Am I?"

I feel anger start to build in me. At a minimum I thought Father Ephrem would understand my situation. Instead, he tries to throw my beliefs under the bus. I pull a napkin from its holder and wipe down an invisible stain on the counter while I compose myself.

"I have walked among those less fortunate than me. I've never flaunted my newfound position. Never asked for money or a favor in return."

Father Ephrem stares at me as his burgers go unattended.

"Since the accident I've strived to be extremely charitable and kind to others, even selling some of my stuff to help the less fortunate. So, why couldn't I be a living saint, and why couldn't I be in the position to execute a miracle?"

We stare at each other until a high-pitched siren distracts us. We eye the grill area, now filled with smoke from the over-cooked burgers.

"Blast it!" Father Ephrem says.

He heads toward the fire extinguisher, and I follow. I take one step, and the scene switches.

I'm back in my vision, but much closer to the structure on fire. I can barely breathe through the acrid smoke, and the screams overwhelm me. Still, the building seems familiar.

"Help!"

I recognize the cry, and I search for its source. In a small window at the base of the structure I see Edie's face, black from the smoke that billows around her.

"Save us!"

Us?

The smoke clears for a second, and I see Charlie's face, red and blistered, silently pleading for rescue.

Concentrate, Saint Bob, says a disembodied voice in my vision.

I'm back in the same position – head and arms raised to the sky.

You can do this, Bob, says a second voice.

I'm no longer alone. Two shadowy figures stand on opposite sides of me, hands on my shoulders. I feel stronger, more confident than in previous versions. I stretch my fingertips to their furthest limit. I hear the loud roar and smell fresh air. The sky cracks, shatters, and eye-searing white envelops everything.

I'm back in the cafe, and the griddle is on fire. Father Ephrem tries to put it out with the extinguisher, but he seems overwhelmed.

I grab the extinguisher and push him aside. I press the trigger, and foam explodes from the cone onto the flames. I feel gentle pressure on my shoulders, my confidence builds, and I move closer to the conflagration.

"Bob, stop!"

I hear Father Ephrem's shout, but I press on, even though the extinguisher gets lighter every second. Yet, no matter how many times I think I'm about to run out of foam, it continues to flow from the nozzle.

It takes five minutes to put the fire out, and by then the First Responders arrive with the proper equipment. Firefighters take my place, and I drop the extinguisher on the floor.

"Bob?"

I turn around. Father Ephrem stares at me, his face covered with soot. He comes to my side, picks up the extinguisher, and presses the trigger. A tiny fizzle of flame retardant squirts out.

"What the –?"

He looks at the extinguisher, and then at me. It's no longer a gaze of mild frustration. Now it contains an element of wonder.

"Maybe I should reconsider this whole living saint thing after all," he croaks out.

I can't sleep. The afternoon's events and the evolving vision keep my mind spinning. I try warm milk to calm me down. It gives me gas. And the hot tea I consume makes me pee more times than normal. I even flip on the television in an attempt to make myself drowsy. No amount of reality shows and infomercials help.

I make a loop of my small apartment — kitchen, bedroom, living room, bathroom, repeat. I find several cobwebs, some mouse droppings, and a cracked toilet seat, but no answers on what happened to me at the cafe.

The extinguisher was empty, despite the fact a plentiful stream of retardant flowed from it while in my hands. I had four new people in my vision—two I needed to save and two more who seemed to guide me in putting out the fire. Instead of being surer of myself, especially since Father Ephrem's acknowledgment of something unique about the incident, I feel totally lost.

During one of my loops I make a side trip to the computer to do some research on saints. I've done this numerous times already but never examined what they achieved to earn their position. The only thing I learn—there are a heck of a lot of saints throughout history.

I pass the bathroom again, gaze at the sink, and stop. The bottle of sedatives Dr. Cosmas prescribed sits near the faucet. I can't recall why I filled the prescription nor why I decided to leave it out instead of putting it in the medicine cabinet. Perhaps I suspected its usefulness at some point in time.

I pop the bottle open, grab a capsule, and wash it down with a cupped handful of water. I glimpse myself in the mirror—bloodshot eyes, puffy cheeks, a bit of soot that didn't come off my skin even after several scrubbings.

"Time for bed."

I don't head into my bedroom. Instead, I grab a pillow and blanket and lay down on the sofa, which I tend to find more comfortable. I switch off the light, close my eyes, and pray for the medicine to take effect.

"Help!"

I'm standing near the corner of the structure, looking into the small basement window. Edie screams for assistance, and Charlie stands beside her, even redder and more blistered than in the afternoon.

"I'll save you," I scream with more assurance than I've felt before.

Concentrate, Saint Bob.

My head and hands are raised to the sky, and the hands of my new companions provide needed strength. I reach my fingertips as far as they can go, hear the roar, smell the fresh air, and watch the sky crack above the structure. It shatters, and a circle of white brilliance emerges.

I take in the opening and am nervous.

"I can't do it," I whisper to my companions.

"Yes, you can," answers one of them. "I've always known you could."

"I know now," says the other companion, "and I should've realized it before."

I turn to my right. Father Ephrem smiles at me, his hand firmly gripping my shoulder.

"Why do you think I never called them dreams, Saint Bob?"

To my left, Dr. Cosmas beams at me.

"Saint Bob, help!" Edie screams my holy name—something she has never called me before.

"You saved me once," says Charlie with a cracked voice. "Now save me again."

Dr. Cosmas and Father Ephrem.

I recall something I read a few hours ago during my research.

St. Cosmas and St. Ephrem!

I examine both of them. They radiate a beautiful golden glow.

The fire rages, the screams continue, and the structure starts to collapse, yet, I feel a joy build in me.

"I know what to do."

My vision self bends an index finger and thumb to resemble a trigger. He points into the center of the hole and fires.

Sunlight filters through the blinds and shines into my eyes. My blanket isn't tangled around me, and I'm not drenched in sweat. I feel refreshed for the first time in months. I glance at the kitchen clock and gasp.

"Oh, my gosh, I'm late."

I shower, dress, grab the extinguisher from under the kitchen sink, and race out the door.

"No, I'm not going to leave," Edie says with arms crossed in defiance. "And neither should you. It's Charlie's first AA meeting, and he needs all the support he can get."

"Well, I'm not really sure you should be here," Charlie says. He looks and sounds healthier than he did when I last saw him on the bar stool.

"I don't care," Edie says to him. "I'm not going to let you deal with this on your own. Oh, and why the hell do you have a fire extinguisher, Bob?"

"I'll need it later."

"For what?"

"An event that's going to happen, which is why I need you and Charlie to leave."

I survey the coffee shop's expansive basement room as people continue to pour in and convene around the coffee makers and boxes of donuts in the little kitchenette area. Wooden tables and chairs are scattered across the rest of the space.

Edie takes a step toward me, her steely gaze bores into my skin. I stand my ground.

"We're. Staying," she says through thin lips.

She turns to Charlie to stare at him. He shrugs.

"Guess I'm staying," he says. "She'd tackle me if I didn't."

"Let's get started, folks."

I whip around and see Father Ephrem in the front of the room.

"Father, you have to leave." I cross the room in long strides.

"Bob? Why are you down here?"

"Please leave, Father."

"Why?"

"The vision. It's coming true. Today."

"Bob, calm down," he says and tries to comfort me with a hand on my shoulder. "When?"

"I'm not really sure, but it's sometime soon."

"All right, how about this? I'll try to cut AA meeting short and have everyone quickly exit. Will that make you feel better?"

"No, but if it's the best you can do ..."

"You have my word," Father Ephrem says.

"Well, if I can't believe a man of the cloth ..."

Father Ephrem smiles and calls for everyone to sit down.

"It's pretty chilly down here," Father Ephrem says to one of the attendees. "Go upstairs and ask them if they can start the fireplace."

I take another look at Edie and Charlie. She returns a glare that I turn away from.

Outside, I take in a breath of fresh air, cross the street, and head into the community garden. I examine all the colorful new blooms, but it does nothing to ease my tension, and I continue to glance every few seconds at the coffee shop. The fire extinguisher hangs heavy at my side.

"Bob?"

I turn around and see Dr. Cosmas behind me.

"I didn't know you liked this garden," she says.

"I normally don't, but I feel like I need to linger here for a while."

"I see." She looks down at my hand. "Bob, why do you have a fire extinguisher?"

I'm about to answer when a concussion of air and a loud explosion blow me and Dr. Cosmas off our feet. We scrabble up and look across the street. Smoke pours from the basement windows of the coffee shop. And not just a grease fire or one spurred on by alcohol. An explosion has taken out a portion of the building and flames shoot high into the sky. Those not caught in the explosion race out the back and front doors, screaming and running every which way.

I try to race toward the scene, but Dr. Cosmas pulls me back.

"What do you think you're doing, Bob?"

"Creating a miracle," I answer and pull away from her.

I sprint across the street, but the heat from the explosion is too intense for me to make it much further. Flames engulf more of the building's exterior every second.

"Help!"

Despite the surrounding cacophony, I hear Edie's cry loud and clear. I step toward the coffee house and am pushed back by flame and thick smoke. I feel the weight in my hand, and I glance down at the fire extinguisher.

"Concentrate, Saint Bob."

The voice comes from above me. Two wispy figures shimmer in the sun.

"We will guide you," says the image of Saint Cosmas.

"Be prepared," says the image of Saint Ephrem.

I put the extinguisher down and stretch my fingertips to touch the figures. They reach out and make contact. I feel confidence bubble inside my soul. I release my hold, grab the extinguisher, move forward into the heat and flame, and press the trigger.

It's not a simple stream of retardant that comes out of the nozzle. Instead, an immense wave of foam measuring several feet wide and high emerges from the small piece of equipment. It encases the coffee shop like some sort of blanket and extinguishes the flames like they are candles on a birthday cake.

I remove my hand from the extinguisher's trigger and drop to my knees. The foam around the coffee house dissipates within seconds. All that remains from the event is a large hole in the building near the basement's fireplace. Not even a wisp of smoke emerges.

I hear the wail of sirens off in the distance and feel a pair of gentle hands lift me from the ground.

"My God, Bob, you were right after all," Dr. Cosmas whispers. "You *can* perform miracles."

"Apparently," I say in a shaky voice. With her guidance I pick up the extinguisher, walk across the street, and push through the group of people gathered near the coffee shop. I hear more loud voices and see a wave of people squeeze themselves out of the ruined building.

"Get the hell out of my way!" Edie shoves herself through the crowd with Charlie behind her.

"Edie!" I wave the extinguisher above my head.

She sees me, races toward where I stand, and bear hugs me to near breathlessness. Charlie merely slaps me on the back.

"A gas leak in the fireplace, I think," Edie says, her voice shrill. "It exploded, and we got pushed to the opposite end of the room. I screamed for help."

"I heard you," I reply.

"From where?"

I point to the gardens across the street.

"How in the Lord's name did you hear me from there?"

"Exactly," I say.

"Huh?"

"Excuse me, Saint Bob?"

I glimpse Father Ephrem behind Edie. A wide smile crosses his features.

"I think you and I need to talk when things quiet down," he says.

"Yeah, I guess so," I say a bit sheepishly.

"What does he mean?" Charlie asks.

"Bob put out the fire by himself," Dr. Cosmas says, eyes still wide at what she just witnessed.

"How in God's name did he do that?"

"Exactly, Charlie," I say and hand him the fire extinguisher.

"You put out an entire building covered in smoke and flames with that?" Edie asks.

"Yep."

"How?"

"Like I told you before, Edie ..." I pause for dramatic effect, "... practice, practice, practice."

Coffee and Kismet

"I swear, if I don't get into law school, I'm gonna work at a crayon factory."

"Kind of harsh, don't you think?" I asked Jeanette, my plutonic-and-that's-all-we'll-ever-be friend.

"I have to leave all my options open, don't I?"

"Sure." I lifted my mug of chai high enough to hide my emerging smirk.

"You're smirking, Tony."

"How the hell do you know that?"

"You always raise your cup to your lips when you think I'm saying something silly."

I shook my head in resignation. Sometimes knowing each other for the length of time Jeanette and I did results in a lack of private grins and eye rolls.

"I'm serious about this law thing," she said.

"I know you are. You've talked about the LSATs since high school."

"But my grades are crap."

"Since when is a 3.5 GPA crap?"

"Well, if you want to get into a decent law school and not one in the Bahamas, you need top grades."

"The Bahamas wouldn't be too bad." I raised my mug again.

"Why do I even bother?" Jeanette raised her hands in a gesture of defeat.

I let her fume a bit and glanced around the café. Jeanette and I discovered it during freshman orientation, and it turned into our regular meeting place for the last four years. Built inside a former cottage, the shop contained small, comfortable rooms which invited you to sip your coffee and stare at the fire or the activity outside its picture windows. I would come by several times a week to observe the actions of other patrons for my sociology project, and Jeanette would meet me after her classes. We would vent our problems and commiserate with each other. Well, Jeanette would vent. I provided most of the commiseration.

"So, why a crayon factory?"

"Hmm?"

"If your crappy grades lead you to fail the LSATs, you said you'd work at a crayon manufacturer."

Jeanette squinted at me—a sure sign I made a remark to raise her ire.

"I think I'd do some good there. Maybe work in their R&D division to create new colors or styles. I always loved to color, remember?"

"Love is probably too weak of a word," I responded. "You were practically obsessed with coloring books."

"Your professional opinion?" Sarcasm dripped from the question.

"I'm studying sociology, not psychology," I answered.

"Yeah, well, I needed something to do to keep my mind off of, you know ..."

I nodded and let her drift off into her own thoughts. Jeanette's childhood wasn't the best, and we tried to avoid bringing it up. Unfortunately, I tended to broach the subject much too often.

"So, how's Dan?" I asked to change the topic.

"Oh, like you care," More sarcasm from Jeanette.

"Just making sure things are copasetic between you two."

"Okay, I guess. He showed up with a black eye and a bloody lip on our last date. He said he got into a fight downtown."

"With his coke dealer, I'm guessing."

"Oh, don't start again. He said he stopped using." Jeanette squinted so tightly I could barely see the whites of her eyes.

"He's using. He basically told me so a few weeks ago."

"What did he say, exactly?" Jeanette's voice dropped into an octave utilized when she needed to pry pertinent information from someone.

"See? Who says you can't be a good lawyer?"

"Spill it, Tony."

"He said, 'Don't tell Jeanette, but I'm still using.'"

"Those exact words?"

"Yup." I smiled.

"And why would he talk to you?"

"Probably high at the time."

"Wow," Jeanette looked at her laptop screen, "that little piece of sh—"

I chuckled at Jeanette's response. I didn't care if I got Dan in trouble. I'd hated him from the moment he stepped into her life the year before. He was a loser with no hope, so I tried to get him in as much trouble with Jeanette as possible, so she would dump him.

"Damn," Jeanette said.

"What?"

"I'm late for my next class." Jeanette slammed her laptop cover down and gathered her belongings. "Don't tell Dan I know about this."

"Right, because we're going to meet for tea and cucumber sandwiches later today."

"You know what I mean, Tony."

"Scout's honor," I answered, raising my palm toward her.

"Didn't you say that in eighth grade before you told Jimmy Parker I liked him?"

I hid a smirk behind my lifted mug of chai.

"Oohhh," Jeanette whirled around and stormed out of the café.

"I swear, if I don't pass the Bar, I'm going to work at a crayon factory."

"Still going with the original plan, I see."

"Always have a backup if everything falls into the toilet," Jeanette said.

"Quite optimistic, I guess."

"You know I'm a realist, Tony. Good fortune doesn't exist. Hard work gets you what you want."

"I'm pretty confident no one else works as hard as you do, Jeannie."

"Damn straight," she replied, tearing into a gluten-free muffin.

I looked away from the devastation of the poor baked good and stared around the café. The furniture was newer, the employees were different, and the students occupying tables laden with tablets and books weren't those Jeanette and I once knew. In fact, they seemed much younger than us when we started college.

With Jeanette in law school and me publishing the findings of my undergraduate sociology project, we didn't come to the café as often. Still, we tried to meet at least once a week, if only for a few minutes, for her to talk and me to nod and provide pithy responses.

"You're going to do fine." I patted her hand for reassurance.

"At least one of you thinks so," she said through a mouthful of muffin.

"Dan's not supporting you?"

"When has that idiot ever supported me?"

"I thought you loved him?" I asked.

"It doesn't mean I still don't think of him as an idiot," she clarified.

She took another bite of muffin and chewed it twenty times before she swallowed. Such a methodical person, yet her choice of men sucked.

"Why do you stay with him?"

"I like bad boys," Jeanette said with a shrug and another bite of muffin.

"Don't give me that crap."

The statement came out more forcefully than I intended, and Jeanette stopped at the fifteenth chew to swallow.

"You're this close to becoming an attorney, Jeannie … an officer of the law. And, being said officer of the law, you'd have to turn him in."

Jeanette stared down at the plate containing the remnants of her snack.

"And I bet he's still using. Oh, sure, he keeps saying he's clean, but I don't see him wearing too many short-sleeve shirts, even in summer."

"And your point is?" she asked into her plate.

"Come on, you're not a stupid person. He's upgraded from cocaine, Jeannie. He's doing heroin, and he doesn't want you to see the track marks."

A pang of guilt shot through me. I commented on Dan countless times, but this time it struck a nerve with her.

"I've read studies on this." I softened my voice to sound conciliatory. "They're afraid or ashamed to let other people know they're using because, they don't know how the hell to stop."

"I—I think there's some good inside him. I think I can change him," she said in a quiet, childlike voice.

"Like you thought you could do with your Dad?"

I didn't mean to say what I did, even though it had remained a thought in my mind for years. I knew about all the difficulties she went through with her parents and the therapy to make her cope. No matter how many times Jeanette said she was over the whole thing, I always felt she bargained with the truth, In the end, Jeanette thought she had the power to fix other people.

Jeanette looked at me without a squint of anger. Then she quietly got up, grabbed her bag, and walked out the door.

"I swear it was a mistake."

"No, Jeanette, it wasn't."

We looked at each other across the café table we'd normally sat at during our time in college. We didn't frequent the place much due to our conflicting schedules and the fact it fell into a bit of disrepair, but we tried to catch up when we could.

"I was drunk, Tony."

"We were both drunk."

"I shouldn't have slept with you."

"I could say the same thing."

"Oh, admit it, Tony. You think about sleeping with me once in a while."

We didn't order any drinks this time around, so I couldn't hide my smirk behind a mug.

"Maybe more than once in a while," I admitted.

"Dammit, I'm getting married next week," Jeanette said.

"Yeah, to Dan."

"What does that mean?" She squinted at me, and I noticed the start of crow's feet around her eyes.

"You tend to ask that a lot," I said.

"Indulge me."

"You're telling me he hasn't cheated on you since you've been dating?"

"He stopped." Jeanette tried to sound confident, but I heard a tone of desperation in her voice. "Just like he stopped using."

"Uh-huh."

She started to speak, and I grabbed her hands.

"Jeannie, I love you."

She pulled away with a jerk. I looked in another direction and cursed myself for finally admitting it to her. I couldn't remember when it went from platonic affection to true love—probably when she began dating Dan. It involved wanting something you couldn't get or some sort of psychological claptrap. Combined with being away from family and old friends it instigated my emotional shift. Somewhere inside I knew my reasons for protecting Jeanette against Dan and the other losers she dated wasn't due to her bad choices. I wanted them to leave, so I could be with her.

"I know." Jeanette whispered so softly I could barely hear her in the continued drone of the café.

"What?"

"I've known for a long time. No member of the opposite sex would defend me so much against the pinheads I've dated if they didn't feel something for me."

She smiled and grabbed my hands.

"But, Tony, it would never work for us. We know each other's idiosyncrasies too well for us to spend a lifetime together."

"I don't have any idiosyncrasies."

"Getting defensive when I say something you don't agree with is one of them."

"I don't get defens—" I paused and took a breath. "Okay, you may have a point, still—"

"I can't let go of what we have now, Tony."

"The typical response," I said.

"I'm going to need you as a sounding board for all the junk that will probably go on after I marry Dan. I need your help to get through it, to get onto the smooth part of the road so he and I can have a life together."

"I'm—I'm not sure I can do that, Jeannie."

"Why?"

"The cat's out of the bag. You know how I feel and the emotions I'll experience when you talk to me about your honeymoon, your sexual problems, and what color you should paint the nursery. I'll place myself in those scenarios, get pissed off I'm not the most important man in your life, and not be the stable sounding board I've been for so many years. In fact, I'll probably give you bad advice to make things fall apart."

"Well, at least you're honest."

"I wouldn't be if I didn't love you."

"So, what then?" The desperation returned to Jeanette's voice.

"I think we need to step away from each other."

Blood left Jeanette's face while she comprehended the words.

"Get married, establish a life with Dan, and make sure he's the one you really want."

I walked over to her side of the table, gave her a kiss on the cheek, and walked out of the café with the taste of salt on my lips.

"I need some money," Jeanette demanded.

"How did you know I was here?" I asked.

"Oh, please."

Despite the tension between us, I smiled. Jeanette and I returned to semi-speaking terms once again and met from time to time at the coffee shop. And even though it continued to disintegrate due to the neglect of the current owners, it remained a sanctuary away from the machinations of the college's administrative politics.

"I'm guessing it has something to do with Dan?"

The intense look on Jeanette's face crumpled, and she plopped herself on a nearby stool.

"I swear," she said softly, "if I didn't have the patience of a saint ..."

"What did he do now?"

"He, er, got into an unfortunate incident."

"And now he's in jail, right?"

"You know, you've gotten cynical over time," Jeanette said.

"Really? I wonder why," I responded.

"And sarcastic."

I pulled at my face with my hand.

"Why can't you afford to bail him out?" I asked.

"Higher amount," she admitted, "because, you know, of the repeat offenses."

"Man should be in prison," I said.

"He's not a bad—"

I raised my hand to stop her comment.

"I guess you're a little low on funds."

"Hey, those of us in the legal defense office don't get paid much working for the county," Jeanette admitted.

"Uh-huh."

A strained silence hung between us like a concrete partition. In the past we enjoyed the quiet times, though there weren't many. Now, I internally pleaded for some type of distraction.

"How much?" I acquiesced.

She sighed in relief and slid her tablet across the table. The screen displayed the bail amount. My eyes widened at the number.

"I just need half of it in cash," Jeanette said to calm me down. "I can get a bond for the rest of the amount."

I looked at her and felt something toward Jeanette I never did before – anger, and the sense I was being manipulated. I provided my digital confirmation to transfer funds with a fingerprint and slid the tablet back.

"Thank you so, so, much."

Jeanette touched my hand, and I jerked it away. She looked down at the tabletop, then at me. The features on her face went from crumpled to crestfallen.

"I have work to finish," I mumbled.

"I'll find a way to pay your back, I swear," Jeanette said.

"Right. Sure. See ya."

She got up, started to walk out, turned to look back at me. She left after I didn't provide any type of acknowledgment.

"Dan's dead."

"What?"

Jeanette grabbed the edge of the table for support and eased herself into the chair opposite mine. Pale with dark circles around her eyes, she looked worse than the decayed surroundings around us at the old coffee shop.

"How? When?"

"He died two weeks ago."

I opened my mouth to ask why she hadn't contacted me sooner, but she stopped me with a raised palm.

"You have your own worries right now, Tony, what with you leaving your professorship and problems between you and your wife."

"We're separated."

A mirthless chuckle came out of Jeanette. "Not surprising. I never liked her anyway."

"I'm pretty sure she felt the same way about you," I confirmed.

She sniffed and pulled a napkin from the dispenser to wipe her nose.

"Forget about that," I said. "How did he die?"

"He never stopped using, Tony. He just got so good at hiding it I never knew, never saw anything around the apartment." Jeanette wiped away tears. "Cocaine and ecstasy—the asshole freebased them together, shot up, and died of a massive heart attack."

"God." I grabbed Jeanette's hands. They shook under my touch.

"I'm a damn idiot, Tony." She allowed the tears to flow freely down her cheeks. "I never believed you, and I whipped myself into a state of denial thinking everything was okay between me and him."

"You're not clairvoyant."

"No, but like you once said, I'm an officer of the law." She blew her nose and straightened in her chair. "I should've smartened up a long time ago."

"Look, Jeannie, just because I'm always right doesn't mean you need to beat yourself up." I smiled, and a shadow of a grin crossed her face. "It's all in the past. Now you have to deal with your future."

"Yeah, well, that's another reason why I took so long to come to you. See, I'm leaving."

My stomach lurched and my heart thudded. The sounds of conversations, coffee machines, and clacking silverware got washed away by the rush of blood to my head. We hadn't been close since she started to ask for money to bail Dan out. Still, over time, the wounds began to heal enough to start communicating a little. Some recent moments felt like we were back in college.

"I can't be here anymore, Tony. I've caused too much pain to a lot of people."

"You didn't do anything," I whispered.

Jeanette reached over and caressed my cheek.

"I swear, Tony, sometimes you're such a lovable guy, but you know what you said is a load of crap. God, I've been terrible to you over these last few years. It was all about me—"

"It was always about you, even before you married Dan."

She chuckled.

"I was selfish, Tony, and unfeeling, and had some kind of Mother Teresa thing going on where I felt I could pull Dan from his inner demons and make him whole again. In fact, I think I spent more time trying to fix him than I did my Dad."

"You loved Dan more," I said.

"I guess," she answered. "I didn't realize how miserable it made me. Here I go being selfish again – thinking more of my feelings than the fact Dan is dead."

"So, where are you going?" I asked.

"Don't know. Maybe somewhere entirely different in this world. I need time to figure out what the hell went wrong in my life and the best way to fix it."

"Are you coming back?"

Jeanette shrugged.

"I'll be here when you do." I looked around the crumbling features of the café. "Well, maybe not here exactly, but ..."

Jeanette nodded and stood.

"Do you still love me?"

"Yes," I replied.

"Do you think that's what caused your separation?"

"Very much so."

"Do you think your wife knew?"

I smiled.

Jeanette snorted. "Yet another thing I screwed up."

She walked out of the room. Despite it full of rowdy college students, the café seemed incredibly empty.

"I swear, if I don't pass the LSATs, I'm going to work at a cosmetics factory."

I smiled at the frustrated college student as I placed a heaping plate of nachos in the center of her table.

"Pretty radical, don't you think?" asked her male tablemate.

"Well, gotta leave all my options open, don't I?"

Memories of a long ago conversation washed over me, and I laughed as I made my way back toward the café's kitchen. Along the way I looked around the cozy room and at all the renovations I'd made after I purchased the café not long after I left the college. I never regretted quitting and starting a second career. Despite the changes I made and the new generation of college students who graced the café's tables, the place felt like home.

I walked down the hallway to the kitchen and examined the works of art along the wall. They were from students of the neighborhood elementary school and burst with colors from, what seemed like, every crayon in a pack. I stopped at one framed picture with swirls of brown, red, and green.

"Creamy Latte. My best creation."

I took an inhalation of breath at the sound of the voice behind me and turned.

"Jeanette?"

She smiled and pointed at the picture.

"This one is Aspen Green, if I recall. One of my first designs."

I continued to stare at her. Two years had passed since she'd left. Two lonely years for me, yet it seemed good for her. Shadows no longer circled her eyes, and her features seemed smoother.

"These are for you," she said.

I looked down. Jeanette held a brand new carton of crayons in her hand.

"Just off the factory line." she said. "Brand new colors. Most of them mine, of course."

I returned my gaze back to her features. I'd always had a witty response to her comments. At that moment I couldn't think of one thing to say.

"You with anyone right now?" she asked.

I shook my head no.

She handed me the crayons, reached into her bag, and pulled out a pile of clean, white paper.

"Let's color," she said with a smile, "and you can talk about your love for me again."

*"Coffee gives me warmth, waking, an unusual force
and a pain that is not without very great pleasure."*
Napoleon

I Married the Hell Outta Her

My blind date walked into the coffee shop two minutes before I finished watching the hell outta of a show on my tablet. I got angry until I looked up and saw she was a smokin' hot babe. I committed at that point to flirt the hell outta her.

It worked. She talked a lot, and I ignored the parts that weren't about me. Then, when she asked me a question, I turned it around and complimented the hell outta her. She smiled, I asked her to sleep with me at that moment, and she slapped the hell outta my face.

Still, we slept together, and after that I courted the hell outta her. I bought her flowers, candy, super-sized meals at McDonald's—whatever I could do to make her love the hell outta me. She fell for it, I fell for her, and I proposed to her during the commercial break of a Stanley Cup game.

I'll be honest, I married the hell outta her. Rockin' DJ, kegs, inviting all her deadbeat relatives—I gave her everything she wanted for the wedding and reception. Then we spent a week in Atlantic City. She broke the hell outta me and I maxed out a few credit cards, but I loved the hell outta her, especially in the sack.

We bought a house in the suburbs, I got a real job, and I impregnated the hell outta her. We had two kids, one of each, and they pooped and peed the hell outta their diapers. I bought a mower and garden tools and landscaped the hell outta my lawn.

Then my manager promoted the hell outta me. I got a corner office, a company car, and a secretary. She was a smokin' hot babe, and I committed at that point to romance the hell outta her. And it worked. I continued to love the hell outta my family, but I banged the hell outta my secretary on the side.

She wanted me to get the hell outta my marriage, but I said no. I mean, why the hell would I want to get outta such a sweet deal? My secretary got angry, went to my house, and spilled the hell outta her guts to my wife.

I came home, we argued, scared the hell outta the kids, and trashed the hell outta the house. My wife threw my stuff into the front yard, and a few weeks later she divorced the hell outta me. A few weeks after that my boss fired the hell outta me. A few months after that my former secretary sued the hell outta me for knocking her up.

Now I work at the coffee shop and live in a studio apartment with roaches so big they gross the hell outta me. I still hang out after work and watch the hell outta shows on my tablet, because I don't have a television, let alone electricity, in my apartment. I'm always hopeful for another babe to cross my path so I can date the hell outta her. As long as she has a working shower and hot food, that is. Can't marry the hell outta another smokin' hot chick while hungry and dirty.

Wrestlin' for God

"D'you have a moment to talk, Pastor?"

No I don't, Connor, Julius Constantine thought to himself. *Go away.*

Julius winced at this internal commentary, because it was no way for the Senior Pastor of the First United Methodist Church of Testament to think about one of his congregation.

It's Connor Wilhelm, for Pete's sake, his inner voice whined. *He'll talk your ear off, and you've a whole church to deal with.*

"You okay?" Connor asked while Julius rapidly blinked his eyes.

"Yeah, I'm fine." Julius pushed the guest chair away from his desk with his foot. "Have a seat."

Connor sat in his usual position. Rear end on the lip of the cushion, head bowed down, hands tightly clasped on his lap. Julius knew this as Connor's I-think-I-have-sinned stance, which probably meant the tiniest of infractions.

Great, more nonsense.

"I don't have much time, so let's get right to the issue."

"I got me a heckuva huge religious type of crisis," Connor spoke into his lap.

Oh, Lord.

"Go on," Julius yielded.

"See, God called on me yesterday."

"Excuse me?"

Connor raised his head, moistness around his eyes.

"God talked to me yesterday, right after dinner."

"Were you drinking at the time?"

"A few beers with dinner," Connor said.

"Define a few," Julius said.

"Three. And three more after I ate."

"Okay." Julius swiveled his desk chair back and forth. His inner monologue screamed at him to stop the conversation.

"What did He tell you?"

"He was pretty specific, actually. God wants me to quit my job and join the WWE."

Julius stopped swiveling.

"Join the WWE and wrestle for him," Connor said.

Julius leaned forward.

"I'm gonna wrestle for the Lord."

"Were you watching wrestling at the time God called you?" Julius asked.

"Uh, yeah, course I was."

"And this happened in the midst of drinking."

"Sure, but I also ate somethin', so the food kinda sucked up the alcohol."

"You know this for a fact?" Julius asked.

"Hey, I read, Pastor. I ain't stupid or nothin'."

"Never said you were," Julius confirmed.

Oh, please.

"Let me get this straight. You were on your sofa, drinking and watching wrestling, and the Lord happens to speak to you at that very moment." Julius said. "Does that cover it?"

"Yup." A small smile crossed Connor's face.

Julius pressed himself into the back of his chair.

"Come on, Connor. Let's be honest with each other here. Don't you think that's a bit of a, um, coincidence?"

"Hel—I mean, heck no, Pastor. I think the Lord wanted me

to do this for a while. Me watchin' wrestlin' ... Well, what's that thing that happens by chance?"

"Happenstance?"

Connor's smile broadened. "Yeah, that's it! It's a joyous happenstance."

"You're happy?"

Connor nodded.

"Then, for the love of all that's holy, why do you need to talk to me? I mean, I've got a pretty busy schedule, Connor. In fact, I'm late for—"

"See, Pastor Julius, I need to know if joinin' the WWE goes against some sort of scripture or sumthin'."

"You're kidding," Julius said

"He wants me to wrestle, but is it wrong if I do it for money?"

Julius rubbed his face to avoid screaming in frustration. Connor had made frequent appearances in his office since he became pastor two years before. At first he found the young man tolerable, if not a bit unambitious and confused. Lately, Julius began to get tired of Connor's inane comments on breaking most of the Commandments.

Julius rubbed his face harder to push the last thoughts out of his mind.

"Pastor?" Connor asked.

"Hold on, I'm thinking," Julius answered, harsh inflection in his voice muffled inside his palms.

"It's really important to know, so anythin' you can tell me ..."

"Look, neither God nor Jesus asked anyone to be poor," Julius said. "In fact, they were okay with an individual obtaining wealth as long as they tithed to the church and donated to the less fortunate."

"You sure about that?" Connor asked.

Like he did most days in recent weeks, Julius frowned.

"It's one of the things we study at the seminary, Connor. I don't make these things up."

"Yeah, I guess you don't. I mean, you're a pastor and all, why the heck would you lie about sumthin' like that?"

To get you out of my office?

"Here's the deal—tithe ten percent of your earnings—"

Why are you continuing along this path? Julius asked himself.

"Oh, I'm gonna donate much more than that! Well, at least once I get the big money like The Rock or Big Show."

"And they're in the WWE?"

"Yeah, famous, too. Well, The Rock is more famous for his movies now, but Big Show is a huge WWE star. Other wrestlers are on all the commercials and television shows. I wanna make a lot so I can to help others."

"How charitable," Julius said with a big dose of sarcasm. "Still, you know that it may take a long time for you to get into the WWE and become famous like Rock and Big Program."

"Yeah, one month is a long time," Connor said.

"Excuse me?"

"God told me it's gonna happen in one month, at the wrestlin' exhibition at the event center."

Julius raised an eyebrow in curiosity.

"And did God happen to tell you how He intends to make it happen?" he asked.

Connor looked around the room in search of eavesdroppers. He leaned forward in his seat.

"It's a surprise."

"You know I hate surprises," Julius admitted.

"God does, too," Connor said. "Thing is, he doesn't want to ruin it for you."

"There's absolutely nothing wrong with Connor."

Julius grimaced at the diagnosis of Doctor Carlos Luichen, Testament's general physician.

"You don't believe me?" Carlos asked.

"Well—"

"A man of the cloth and you don't believe a member of your own church? Of course, coming from you …"

"It's not that I don't believe you. It's more like I don't believe it."

"The results don't lie, Pastor," Carlos said. "I can show you the CAT Scan and MRI images if you like."

Julius waved a hand across his face. "And what am I supposed to look for?"

"Just hold on a moment, and indulge me and the St. Albert's Medical staff who spent many hours probing Connor's brain."

Carlos placed images of Connor's brain and skull on his light board

"No tumors or abnormal brain activity. In fact, Connor's brain is one of the healthiest I've seen in a long time."

"That's saying something for him."

Carlos turned sharply and ripped one of the scans from the board.

"What the hell do you mean by that?"

"Language, Doctor."

"I don't give a good gall darn about language, Pastor," Carlos said, the last word dripping with disdain. "I know you sometimes act like the religious equivalent of that mean television doctor, but even that statement crossed the line."

Julius looked contemptuously at Carlos, sighed, and bowed his head.

"You're right, sorry."

"Well, sh—, I mean shoot," Carlos said in a quieter tone. "What's going on, Julius?"

Julius felt some of his stoniness begin to crumble.

"Honestly, I'm not sure."

Julius pulled up a stool and sat down heavily.

"Care to talk about it?" Carlos asked.

"I'm usually the one who asks that question."

"Yeah, I'm pretty sure you're not the only religious leader who has said the same thing to another person." Carlos grabbed a chair to sit across from Julius. "Give it to me."

"I'm not feeling very religious lately."

"Big shocker," Carlos said.

"What do you mean?" Julius asked.

"Have you listened to your own sermons lately? I mean, you're not always gentle, but at least you've included something in the past on respect and love for each other. Now, it's almost like you're angry at God or something."

"I'm not angry at Him," Julius said.

"You sure? Even after you said 'I'm not too happy with God' during the last sermon?"

"No, I'm not sure."

"Okay, so what changed?"

"Ditto."

"Let me guess, it's Connor."

"Nah, Connor's a symptom of the problem," Julius admitted. "This funk has been building for weeks. Connor's revelation tipped me over the pulpit."

"Maybe you need a break."

"Right, because Jesus took a vacation from his duties."

"He did die and come back. That's sort of a rest," Carlos said.

"Seriously? You just told me *I* crossed a line."

"Now we're even," Carlos said.

Carlos reached into a nearby drawer and pulled out a small bottle of brownish liquid and two specimen cups. He poured a small amount of the bottle's contents into each cup.

"Those are clean, right?" Julius asked.

"Drink it," Carlos passed a cup toward Julius.

"I don't drink."

"It's medicinal."

"Well, you're the physician …"

The two men toasted each other and drank the liquid in one gulp. Julius gasped for air and began to cough.

"I thought … you said … this was medicinal," Julius stammered.

"It's strong medicine," Carlos said. "Want some more?"

"Absolutely." Julius put out his cup.

Carlos filled it with a smile. "How long have we been friends, Julius?"

"Two years. Since I arrived in Testament."

"Huh, thought it longer than that." Carlos took another swig. "Anyway, I knew you were different than previous pastors during your first church meeting. You had an aura about you, an energy and enthusiasm for God and faith that exuded from your pores, despite your growing caustic attitude. We hadn't seen such motivation for a long time."

"And that energy's gone," Julius admitted.

"It comes in fits and starts," Carlos corrected.

"It scares the hell out of me, Carlos."

"Language, Pastor," Carlos said.

Julius took another drink and examined the cup's remaining contents. "Testament is my first parish."

"Really? Who made that decision?"

"Hey, I go where God points me and where the Rocky Mountain Conference has an opening for a pastor."

"You've done okay so far," Carlos stated.

"I know I've done good, but so far isn't enough for me or for this town." Julius stood and felt the warmth of his drink spread though his body. "Religious leaders don't get to do things halfway and think it'll make things better."

"Even in a podunk town like this one?"

"Testament isn't a podunk town," Julius said with a frown.

"You're right. We have a bed-and-breakfast. That makes us a one horse town."

"Carlos, you have a community here, and you need someone like me to help guide them toward peace and faith."

"And you're the only one that meets the requirements?" Carlos' question dripped with sarcasm.

Julius remained silent.

"Well, Pastor, that's a bunch of bullshit. And, yeah, the term fits."

"You're saying Testament is so stable that you don't need my services?"

"Oh, we still need them," Carlos admitted. "Plenty of folks around here need your guidance, Connor among them. I'm just saying that you're not the Chosen One, and you can't turn water into wine. We do that in the vineyard across the street from the bed and breakfast."

"I never said I was the Second Coming."

"You certainly sound like it at times," Carlos said.

"Gee, thanks."

"I have news for you, Julius—you're human. Yes, you're a man of religion, but it doesn't mean you can't doubt your own faith. Look, I'm sure you've been doing this for a long time …"

"I'm only thirty-five," Julius admitted.

"Wow, I thought you were much older. No wonder you're so unsure." Carlos answered seriously while he lifted the bottle from the counter. "Need another shot?"

"While I'd be honored to drink some more *medicine* with some-one as mature and wise as you …"

"Hey, I'm only forty-five," Carlos said.

"I'm going to head out." Julius tossed the cup into a nearby wastebasket.

"And what are you going to do when you step out my door?" Carlos asked.

"Search my soul for the reason I'm so angry, find the rotten seed, and quickly extract it."

"And if you can't?"

Julius shrugged. "Then I'm not much of a religious leader for Testament, am I?"

"Wow, you look miserable."

Julius looked up. Katie Munson, hostess-server at Hamburger Haven, stood next to his booth.

"I mean, more miserable than normal," she corrected.

"You're a comfort," Julius said. "Ever think of joining the Order?"

"Become a nun? Nah, too much previous sexual baggage," Katie admitted. "My habit would probably disintegrate from all the things I did in my youth."

"I'm sure you've been forgiven." Julius said.

"Who knows? There was a lot of sexual baggage."

Katie sat down opposite Julius and grabbed a fry from his plate.

"Care to talk?" she asked.

"That's my line," Julius responded.

"Not lately. Every time I visit you it's more 'What do you want?'"

"I'm busy."

"Sure, you go and tell yourself that," Katie said.

Julius put down his burger. "You really have the time to hear my issues?"

Katie grabbed another fry. "Business is slow. Spill it."

Julius took a deep breath to begin his confession.

"Hey, there's the future star of the WWE!"

Katie and Julius turned toward the restaurant's entrance.

"Holy cow," Katie gasped. "Look at him."

Julius hadn't seen Connor since he left for Boulder earlier in the month. His former mane of shoulder-length hair no longer existed. Instead, Connor's bald head reflected the restaurant's overhead lights. The small beer-drinking paunch he once displayed no longer existed. Despite being gone for only a few days, Connor's physique resembled the structure of someone who spent several weeks working intense weights and cardio.

"Wow, look at those guns," Katie said in greeting. Julius felt a stab of jealousy when she walked up to Connor and squeezed a bicep that protruded from his t-shirt.

"My, my. I'd sure like to see how that weapon works one day," she said with a smirk. "Let me find you a seat."

"Here, Connor, come take my booth," one of the patrons said.

"Son, come sit with me," commanded another customer.

Soon, everyone in the restaurant wanted Connor to sit next to them.

All except me.

Connor raised his hand. The room went silent in an instant.

"Thanks for all of your invites, but there's one person I need to speak with first."

Connor looked in Julius' direction, and the rest of the restaurant's crowd followed suit.

Oh, come on.

Connor began to walk toward Julius' booth.

Don't sit here. Don't sit here. Don't sit here.

"Pastor Julius, good to see you!"

"You too, Connor. Sit down, I guess."

"Man, I haven't seen you since I left for the trainin' center."

"Yeah," Julius said. "I have to admit, you've really changed."

"Feel changed, too," Connor said. "Eatin' clean, exercisin', no beer in weeks. Probably the healthiest and clear-headed I've been my whole life."

"Oh? Does that mean you've had second thoughts about your plan?"

"You bet."

"And?"

"And I'm one hundred percent sure the Lord wants me to be his herald for the WWE."

"I see."

"Look at me, Pastor." Connor opened his arms wide. "I couldn't have done this by myself. He's helpin' me get in shape."

"Maybe God isn't the only one who helps you."

"I don't get you," Connor said with a frown.

"We all know there are drugs out there that—"

"No way in hell, Pastor Julius!"

The volume of Connor's response silenced the other diners.

"I would never, ever take any type of performance enhancin' drug to do His work. That's against everythin' you taught me."

"You listened to me?" Julius asked.

"Sure."

"But, I barely got a word in when you came to speak with me all those times."

The restaurant crowd continued to ogle them like a car accident with horrendous injuries. Katie crossed her arms and scowled in Julius' direction.

"You don't believe me," Connor said.

"About the drugs or God speaking to you?"

"Both."

"I never said I didn't—," Julius started.

"Come out to Boulder tomorrow, and see how I train."

"Boulder is a little far for me."

Connor slammed a hand on the booth's tabletop. Julius saw anger and something that looked like disappointment Connor's features.

"I'll show you that it's His work, Pastor."

Connor rose and walked out of Hamburger Haven without saying good-bye to anyone. Katie and other patrons turned away from Julius without saying another word.

"You have visitors," the church's secretary said when she poked her head into Julius' office.

Great. More people to stop me from finishing this paperwork.

"Who?" Julius asked dejectedly.

"Katie and Carlos."

"Tell them I'm not here."

"We can hear you," Katie said from the reception area.

"Fine, send them in."

The secretary disappeared, and Katie and Carlos entered. Katie closed the door behind her.

"Private conversation?" Julius asked.

"More like a lecture," Carlos answered.

"Sure, because I always enjoy a talking to by members of my congregation."

"Oh, shut up," Katie said angrily.

Julius' eyes widened at Katie's tone.

Ease up on them, they're not who you're mad at right now.

Julius closed his eyes, exhaled, and refocused his attention on his guests.

"Not going to ask us to sit down?" Carlos asked.

"You know where the chairs are," Julius answered.

Ease up.

"I know you're the handsome religious leader of this dinky little town," Katie began, "but it doesn't give you the right to talk the way to did to Connor at the Haven."

Julius raised an eyebrow.

"You think I'm handsome?"

"Stick with the topic," Katie demanded.

"Fine. I admit it wasn't my greatest counseling session—"

"Christ, Pastor. I'm guessing the angels cringed when they heard you," Carlos said.

"And how did you find out about my talk?"

"The HHDN," Carlos answered.

"The what?" asked Julius.

"The Hamburger Haven Diners Network," said Katie.

Julius shook his head.

"The town's grapevine of chatterboxes," Carlos clarified.

"Right, the snitches," Julius said.

"Wow," Katie murmured.

"What's your problem with the boy?" Carlos asked.

"The Pastor doesn't think God spoke to Connor," Katie answered.

"He hasn't had much good to say about the Lord in his last few sermons," Carlos said.

"That's true, now that you mention it," Katie confirmed.

"Still in the room," Julius said.

"Physically, yes," Katie stated.

"Look, why would God help Connor transform so fast in order to participate in a sport that personifies violence and lies?"

"Why does it bother you?" Carlos asked.

"God doesn't work that way," Julius answered in growing frustration.

"How about Samson or David?" Katie asked.

"Not the same thing," Julius said through clenched teeth.

"And how do you know?" Carlos questioned.

"Because I'm the friggin' Pastor of this friggin' church and should know what God does and doesn't do!"

Yeah, good one. Way to make them trust you.

"I think it's time you both left."

Carlos and Katie remained in their seats while Julius tried to gaze anywhere but in their direction.

"You know, I wasn't one of your biggest fans when you interviewed," Katie said.

"I could've gone either way," Carlos added.

"You seemed too young to take on the position in a close-knit town like Testament where every one of your missteps is broadcast," Katie admitted.

"We're the same age," Julius said.

"Whatever. You turned me around. You're stern, but with a sweet core. You're unyielding, yet compassionate when needed. And you never gave up the fight while we recovered from the wildfires and floods. We wouldn't be the same without you."

"There's a 'but' embedded in this," Julius said.

"But … you're turning into a total asshole," Carlos said.

"You're unsure about your faith, I understand," Katie said.

"How do you know?"

Carlos raised his hand.

"So much for doctor-patient privilege," Julius mumbled.

"You weren't my patient at the time."

"And I guess that's what you were going to tell me at the Haven before Connor stepped in," Katie said.

"Maybe," Julius answered.

"You can't take it out on your parishioners, Julius, especially when they feel God can show them the way," Carlos said.

Julius looked down at the surface of the desk, blurred by the watering of his eyes.

"Are you two done berating me?" he asked in a raspy voice.

Katie and Carlos looked at each other. Carlos nodded.

"Yep, I think so," Katie answered.

They made their way to the door. Katie turned before exiting.

"We've all been where you are now."

"But not with so much at stake."

Katie shrugged. "I was a young hellraiser close to either death or prison. I found the Answer and came out stronger in the end."

"Did you?" Julius asked.

"I'm sober, steadily employed, and feel a connection with God and my pastor," Katie answered with a smile. "What do you think?"

"Connor's a natural."

"A natural what?" Julius asked despite knowing better.

"Athlete," answered Ray 'The Holy Ghost' Needmider, Connor's trainer. "I've never seen someone pick up everything so quickly."

"He watched a lot of wrestling," Julius confided.

"Yeah, people say that to me all the time. Thing is, you can't become a wrestler by watching hours of television. You have to learn a grace almost like, you know, ballet or something in order to do it."

"You're comparing professional wrestling to ballet?"

"Do you have another comparison?" Ray asked.

Julius turned his attention to the center's roped-off ring. Connor, dressed in a skintight unitard, moved counter-clockwise across its padded floor, hands raised in a defensive position against the larger and more muscular opponent he circled. Julius hated to admit it, but a grace did exist in the way the wrestlers moved on the simplified stage.

He noticed a glow surround Connor, and time seemed to slow while Connor made his move. The illumination dissipated, and Connor had his opponent down on the mat.

"See that? Took him down with a half-nelson," Ray said. "Didn't even see him make the move. He's that good."

Julius replayed the moment in his mind and couldn't recall Connor making any type of offensive move toward his opponent.

Divine intervention?

Julius shook his head to clear the silly thought from mind.

"Faith drives him, you know," Ray said.

Julius drew his attention back to the trainer.

"It's what propels him to be the best he can be, Pastor. Not any type of drugs."

"Oh, he said something about that?" Julius asked.

"Wouldn't you if someone pointed an accusing finger?"

"Well, look at him." Julius nodded in the direction of the ring. "Not only has Connor gotten remarkably fit in a short period of time but he's able to take down someone twice his weight."

"So what? Haven't you ever heard of the momentum of a lighter object bringing down something with more density?"

"So you're a physics professor now?" Julius asked.

"You need a basic knowledge of physical properties in order to get these guys to do the things people enjoy watching," Ray stated.

"It's all scripted," Julius said with simmering anger.

"You bet, but at its base is actual technique," Ray said.

"Something Connor has taken to with more enthusiasm than I can remember from my other trainees."

Julius glanced back at the ring. Connor stood while his next opponent climbed through the ropes.

"It doesn't make sense."

"What doesn't?" asked Ray.

"Connor had plenty of religious angst, but no sense of ambition in the two years I've known him. Now he's here because God apparently told him it's his religious destiny to do so."

"He works in mysterious ways," Ray said.

"Yeah, so I've heard."

Julius watched Connor circle his next opponent. The lights brightened for a moment, and Connor had pinned the larger man to the mat.

"I got called by Him," Ray said.

"Excuse me?"

"It doesn't happen only with those in the ministry, Pastor."

"Come on, Ray, I know that, but—"

"I had my own problems at one time. Sure, I wasn't super famous like Hulk Hogan, but I had groupies and dabbled in some extra-curricular activities away from my wife and child. And, yes, I took performance enhancing drugs."

Ray lifted his right sleeve and displayed a scarred track mark that started at mid forearm and ran up his bicep.

"All injections back then. Anyway, things began to look up in my career. I was about to appear in one of the early Wrestle-Mania events where I would go from a second-string antihero to full-on WWE superstar. I shot up with a little steroid cocktail, and my heart stopped not too long after.

"I thought that was it for me. Thing is, in that split second between breathing and excruciating pressure in my lungs, I didn't think about my wife, or child, or any of my other loved ones. Instead, the thought that streaked across my mind concerned the loss of my superstar wrestling status.

"I didn't experience an out-of-body moment or see a white light. Instead, God called from somewhere telling me my time wasn't up. He wanted me to become a guide for all others interested in pursuing an athletic path."

"He told you to teach people how to get into the WWE?"

"Not exactly those words, " Ray said.

"Then how did you know that's what he wanted?" Julius asked.

"How did *you* know?" Ray countered.

Julius opened his mouth to respond, but quickly closed it with a snap. At this moment he didn't really know.

"There're no drugs here, Pastor," said Ray. "Just faith and encouragement, and right now, Connor has the most of both inside him."

"If you say so," Julius answered as Ray made his way to the ring.

Why can't you believe this?

"Because I don't believe in myself anymore," Julius whispered into the air.

"Hey, Pastor," Connor said as he approached Julius. "How d'you think I did?"

"Good, I guess," Julius answered.

"Yeah, you're not a wrestlin' type of guy, are you?"

"No, I meant I don't know. I never saw you make the moves."

"Oh, that. Yeah, I'm pretty fast when I'm ready to attack."

"I've seen turtles outpace you back in Testament," Julius said.

"I more motivated since He looks over my shoulder and makes sure I'm takin' all the right steps."

"If you believe it—"

"So, you comin' next week?" Connor asked.

"Coming to what?" Julius asked.

"The wrestlin' exhibition at the event center, remember? That's not too far from Testament, right?"

"I guess not."

"I'm in the first match. And get this … WWE scouts are gonna be there."

"You sure you're goin' to wrestle for them?"

"Oh, absolutely, 'cept—"

"What?"

"I think He's leavin' out an important part of the plan," Connor admitted.

"I don't understand."

"He got pretty detailed on what I needed to do up to this point. Thing is, there's a big gap between my wrestlin' match and when the WWE accepts me. It's like he's keepin' sumthin' from me."

"He works in mysterious ways," Julius said.

Like when he stopped talking to me.

"I know. Well, maybe I didn' hear Him right. I'll talk with Him again to make sure."

"Yeah, you do that," Julius said.

"Got to shower and talk to Ray. See ya."

Connor smiled, slapped Julius on the shoulder, and ran toward the locker rooms.

Julius walked over to examine all four corners of the empty ring. He climbed the two small steps leading up to the mat, grasped the ropes, and looked around. Nothing seemed mystical or spiritual in the cloth, ropes, and turnbuckles. He lifted his head toward the ceiling and examined the line of fluorescent bulbs across the bare beams. No divine intervention there, only emptiness. Similar to the way he now felt inside.

Why are you talking to Connor but not me?

He jumped down and made his way to the exit. Behind him, the lights faded to black.

Julius used to love to walk the trails through the Testament Memorial Open Space during the early morning hours when it remained fairly empty. For him, the three mile hike to the tip of Partition Rock used to be one of meditation, contemplation, and the period when he and God would converse. He rarely meditated any more during his hikes. Instead, it got replaced by the sound of his own heavy breathing courtesy of the many burgers and fries devoured at Hamburger Haven.

He now hiked the boulder-strewn path out of habit, and sometimes he didn't even get that far. Events of the last few weeks made it hard for him to roll out of bed and start the morning by trudging six miles. In fact, sometimes he felt it better to pull the warm comforter over his head and call it a day. Why deal with Testament's spiritual problems when he couldn't solve his own?

He stopped midway up the path to drink some water and scanned the landscape. Testament's small imprint sat to the east of his position with nearby towns spread between patches of farmland. He squinted and could barely make out the tiny ant-like vehicles moving across the Interstate that divided Colorado between the mountainous west and the flatness of the east.

Julius could see a similar dividing line in his thoughts. On one hand he greatly desired to connect with the Lord again, to feel his love. On the other, he really didn't give two hoots and felt like throwing in the towel.

He made it to Partition Rock and sat cross-legged on its craggy surface to observe brilliant light paint the landscape a warm yellow. Despite his current state of emotions, the site of sunrise boosted his mood enough to prepare him for the day ahead.

"Hello, Lord, it's me again," he said out loud. "Thank you for another beautiful sunrise. On another topic, why aren't you speaking to me anymore?"

A soft breeze swirled around the rock, cooling some of the perspiration on Julius' face.

"I mean, I've sought guidance for weeks now, and you can't find the time to provide a single suggestion on my future path. You'd rather focus your attention toward Connor."

To his ears, the last statement sounded like a jealous ten-year-old whose younger brother got an action figure when he didn't.

"That was wrong to say, Lord, but I don't apologize. You called me to be your voice in the world. You asked that I be Testament's spiritual advisor, the rock they lean on when they reach a crossroads in their own faith or when they need counseling. How the heck can I guide them if I have problems of my own?"

Julius heard nothing but the rustle of the wind on some nearby brush.

"Tell me, Lord, is it supposed to be this way? Is there a point in your servants' lives when they need to show their loyalty to you? Is this a test? I'm failing pretty badly right now if that's the case. How about letting me in on what you think? Can we talk this out, or should I give it up and do … well, I'm not sure what the hell I would do? Of course, you're not available, so …"

"Pastor Julius uses another swear word. Well, the world is going to come to an end now."

Julius turned at the voice and saw Katie walk toward him.

"I'm allowed five of them a year," Julius said.

"According to who?" Katie asked.

"The Methodist Conference, or at least some of the older pastors in the conference."

"Ah, word of mouth. Glad to see misinformation still reigns in religious circles."

"You have the HHDN," Julius said. "We have the CGN, The Conference Gossip Network."

"To find out which pastor is taking from the offering plate, I guess," Katie said.

"Don't get smart."

Katie sat down next to Julius and pulled a energy bar from her backpack.

"Don't see you here much at the crack of dawn," Julius said.

"Day off," Katie said through a mouthful of fruit and oats. "I try to get up here during my free days."

"I didn't realize you had any free days from the restaurant."

"You don't realize a lot about me, Julius."

"I guess not."

Julius noticed how the sunlight reflected off Katie's hair. He felt a growing smile crease his features.

"I'm guessing you weren't talking to yourself," Katie said.

Julius' smile faded.

"I was speaking with God, or trying to speak with Him."

"Uh-huh," Katie said after a swallow of water. "You two still not on talking terms?"

"He's not interested in answering," Julius said.

"Are you sure it's Him who has the problem?" Katie asked.

"What do you mean?"

"Maybe He's tried to get in touch with you, but you don't hear Him."

"Come on, Katie, it's the Lord. I could hear Him under water or buried deep in this mountain if he desired."

"Why would you be buried in the mountain?"

"My point is—"

"How're you feeling lately?" Katie asked.

"Besides the fact I'm losing my faith?"

Katie nodded.

"Fine," Julius said.

"Besides the Connor issue and the faith thing."

"Fine." Julius said firmly.

"You sure? You look tired."

"I'm not getting enough sleep," Julius said.

"Or too much," Katie countered. "You're making more visits to the restaurant than you used to."

"I'm hungry."

"And your conversations are terse and sometimes a little nasty," Katie said.

"Lots on my mind."

"And the sermons ..."

Julius stayed silent.

"Are there times you don't want to get out of bed?"

Julius stared at her.

"Or not deal with any people?"

Julius dipped his head to his chest.

"Or not been able to clear the weight off your shoulders or the fog from your head?"

Julius returned his attention to Katie.

"You need to see Doc Carlos," Katie said while she packed up her belongings.

"Why?" Julius asked.

"Because your silence answered my questions. Go see him, and tell him how you're feeling." She stood and shouldered her backpack. "By the way, when are you picking me up?"

"For what?"

"Connor's exhibition. He invited me. You are taking me, right?"

"Um ..."

"Go to Carlos, and pick me up after you do that. We can go about realizing each other on the ride to the event center."

She turned, and Julius felt a surge of desire in the way Katie's hair swayed across her shoulder blades.

"You're depressed."

Julius looked at Carlos like he had spoken a foreign language. "I don't understand."

"Boy, you've been saying that a lot lately. All the signs are there, Pastor—change in sleeping and eating patterns, mood swings, unsocial behavior, feelings of dread and uncertainty. There are at least ten items on the list that determine if a person is experiencing depression. You fit most of them."

"How?"

"Lack of serotonin development in your brain or low vitamin D. However, I'm guessing it has to do with stress."

"Stress causes depression?"

"Hell … Heck, yes, Julius. You spend countless hours running your head off to help the folks in and around Testament. Combined with bad food and other factors, even the Pope would be knocked for a loop."

Carlos walked to his desk and opened a drawer.

"Not the brown liquid again," Julius said.

"Nope. You don't need that type of medicine anymore."

Carlos pulled out a prescription pad, scribbled something on it, and passed the torn-off portion to Julius.

"Get this filled. It might take a few weeks until you feel the full effects."

Julius examined the illegible writing scrawled across the paper.

"Your writing sucks," he said.

"Thanks for the compliment," Carlos retorted.

"Do you think it'll help me talk with God again?"

Carlos shrugged.

"I'm only a doctor. That's between you and the Lord to sort out."

"Someone's waiting for you."

Julius' secretary mentioned this before he turned the corner toward the church's reception area.

"In my office?" he asked.

"Nope, main chapel," she answered.

"Care to tell me who it is?"

"It's a surprise." she said with a smile.

"You know I don't like surprises," Julius said.

"Yep."

Julius acquiesced and headed toward the chapel, dropping the pharmacy bag on his office desk.

The quiet of the sanctuary area engulfed him as he padded to the front pew where his guest sat. In the last steps Julius realized he recognized the person from the bald head and broad shoulders.

"Connor?"

Connor turned and gave Julius a huge smile.

"Hey, I didn' know when you were gonna be back, so I came to the chapel to do some prayin'."

"About tonight?" Julius asked.

"Some, but mostly prayers for you."

"Me?"

"Oh, yeah, Pastor. I've noticed you've lost faith. At first I thought it was me."

"Yeah." Julius sat next to Connor. "You're definitely a pain, Connor, but it turned out to be something else."

"What?"

"Tell you another time."

"Okay. Well, I realized sumthin' after our talk at the Haven. We're doing the same thing for the Lord."

"Huh?"

"I'm wrestlin' for God, Pastor, but you're wrestlin' for God's attention."

Julius leaned against the pew's wooden back.

"You were never this intuitive before, Connor."

"Got some more smarts after God called." He rose and made his way out of the row. "So, you're comin' tonight, right?"

"I'll be there with bells on," Julius said.

"Great. I also asked Katie to go."

"She already asked me to pick her up."

"Oh, good. By the way, I know the part He forgot to tell me."

"You do?"

Connor nodded.

"Care to let me in on the secret?" Julius asked.

"It's a surprise," Connor answered.

"I don't like surprises."

"Yep," Connor responded.

"This looks fun," Katie said excitedly while she observed the activity in the event center.

"I assumed that's why you came," Julius said.

"I did it because Connor asked me to."

"And do you always do what Connor requests of you?" Julius asked.

"Have you seen him lately? The man's built like a small mountain," Katie said.

"There is that."

Katie smiled, and Julius returned the expression. It felt good, natural. The depression medication didn't cure him outright. Instead, the first dose made him a little giddy, giving Katie impetus to glance at him crookedly a few times when he broke out in giggles.

"Maybe he asked you to invite me because God told him about your admiration of my hair up at Partition Rock."

Julius blushed.

"Hey, the fact you're a Pastor doesn't mean you can't admire a woman," Katie said, "or her luxurious hair."

Julius smiled and looked around to avoid Katie's gaze. The event center's seats were filled for the exhibition. He and Katie sat ringside beside several rowdy fans with painted faces and signs.

"Did Connor mention something about a WWE scout?" Julius asked Katie.

"Not that I recall," she responded. "Why?"

"Well ..."

"Ladies and gentleman," the ring announcer proclaimed, "welcome to an evening featuring Colorado's best professional wrestlers. At stake is recognition as one of the top and most powerful wrestlers in the state."

A small round of applause echoed across the center while the fans next to Julius screamed at the announcer to move it along.

"First on the ticket, a contest between a new wrestler trained by Ray "The Holy Ghost" Needmider and a returning champion from the Southwest Colorado Wrestling Conference.

Two spotlights appeared on opposite sides of the arena.

"On your left, weighing in at 235 pounds, is the SCWC's Gold Belt Champion, Douglas Killheart!"

A large man emerged and proceeded to make his way toward the ring, the spotlight following him and his entourage.

"Holy crap, he's huge," Katie said.

"Hey, language," Julius said.

"Sure, that's gonna happen here."

"On your right," continued the announcer, "weighing in at 215 pounds, please welcome Connor "The Holy Messenger" Wilhelm!"

"The Holy Messenger?" Katie asked with a raised eyebrow.

"Wooo!" Julius clapped his hands hard and wondered why he had shouted in such a way. Connor came down the aisle next to his row of seats. To Julius he looked confident and unnerved. Behind him, Ray walked slower and seemed a bit pale.

"Does Ray seem okay to you?" Julius asked.

"Who?" Katie countered.

"Connor's trainer."

"Never met him. Kill him. Connor," Katie shouted when he made his way into the ring.

"Hey, did he invite anyone else in town?" Julius asked.

"Man, you're asking a lot of questions," Katie answered. "No one mentioned it at the Haven. I'm happy he invited us."

Julius tried to discern a reason for the lack of Testament supporters but became distracted once the wrestlers went to their corners and the announcer left the ring. An electronic bell buzzed to signify the start of the round.

Killheart moved first with an attempt to slam into Connor by bouncing off the ropes and slamming him with a forearm. Connor anticipated this and ducked under the arm, bouncing off another set of ropes, and drop-kicking Killheart in the chest. Connor's opponent fell to his knees but returned to his feet before the referee could check on him. In turn, Killheart grabbed Connor's skull and began to apply pressure with his fingers.

"Clawhold," Katie yelled. "Break out of it, Connor!"

Julius examined the lights along the center's ceiling. None of them glowed with extra luminance.

Not this time, came a powerful voice inside Julius' head.

Lord?

Just watch, my son.

Connor began to sink to the mat, then grabbed hold of Killheart's wrist and twisted. The clawhold released, Connor spun around Killheart. Grip firmly on Killheart's wrist, Connor leapt off the mat, holding Killheart, and crashed to its surface.

A collective "Oooo" coursed through the crowd as Killheart writhed in pain. Connor leapt again and slammed his knee down into his opponent's solar plexus. Another "Oooo" erupted from the crowd, followed by a rally cry for The Holy Messenger.

"Come on, Connor," Julius said through gritted teeth. He glanced at Katie as she rooted Connor on. She turned, gave Julius a fiercely pleasurable look, and tightly grabbed onto his hand. He felt a rush of warmth course through his body.

Connor attempted to pin Killheart, but his opponent took the advantage and flipped him over. Killheart stood and wrapped his arm around Connor's neck as the young man began to sit up. Connor avoided the sleeper hold, reached up with his free arm, and flipped Killheart over him.

"How the hell did he do that?" Katie asked.

"Physics," Julius answered, now standing to root on the man he once thought a kind but unambitious individual.

Connor tried to pin Killheart again, but he rolled away, stood, and made his way to the ropes. Killheart climbed to the top turnbuckle and performed a backward somersault. Connor saw this in time and rolled out of the way. Killheart slammed into the mat with a reverberating crash and lay immobile.

"Finish him, Holy Messenger," Julius shouted.

"Give him the Last Rites," Katie added.

"Last Rites! Last Rites!" came the cry from people around Julius and Katie. In seconds the mantra spread across the rest of the arena.

"We're trend setters," Katie shouted.

Killheart began to stir. Connor climbed on the top rope and waited until his opponent reached a kneeling position. He leapt, wrapped his arm around Killheart's head, and swung himself backward in mid-air.

"My God," whispered Julius.

Not me, my son. All Connor, said the powerful inside voice that made Julius take a step back.

Connor landed back first, forcing Killheart's head into the mat. With the crowd on their feet, Connor flipped his dazed opponent on his back, planted his body across Killheart's shoulders, and waited for the referee to count to ten.

"Ten!" shouted the referee as the bell rang.

The crowd went crazy around Julius, except for the face-painted fans nearby. They seemed heartbroken that their favorite wrestler lost to a newbie like Connor.

"He did it," said Katie. "Holy God, he did it."

She grabbed Julius' face in her hands and kissed him hard on the lips. Her eyes opened wide as she pulled away.

"I, um, sorta wanted to do that for a long time," Katie said.

"You berated me, now you kiss me." Julius smiled. "I'm getting mixed signals here."

"Please be quiet."

She moved in for another kiss but missed when Julius turned his head toward the ring.

"Seriously," Katie said, "that berating thing—"

"Something's wrong."

Julius noticed the way Ray stumbled toward Connor rather than leaping for joy at his victory. He reached Connor, gave him a bear hug, and slid down to the mat.

"Oh, no," whispered Katie.

The roar of the crowd died down when they noticed the events inside the ring. EMT staffers checked Ray's pulse and breathing. An arena staffer rushed down to the ring carrying a defibrillator.

Julius looked up at Connor, who stood at a respectful distance from the action.

"Why isn't Connor reacting?" Julius asked.

You'll know soon enough, came the voice.

"I don't understa— "

Soon enough, came God's reply.

"Pastor Julius!"

Julius shook himself and returned his focus on the ring. Connor looked directly at him, the announcer's microphone in his hand.

"I need your help," Connor said.

It seemed like the entire crowd now looked at him. Julius turned to Katie. She nodded and squeezed his hand for support. He jogged over to the steps, crawled through the ropes, and stepped over to Ray's unmoving body.

"Pray for him," Connor said in a flat voice.

"Is he dying? I don't have my sacraments," Julius said.

"It's okay," Connor gently said.

You only need your faith, God said.

Julius felt something erupt inside. He gasped and felt a peace he believed he'd lost a long time ago. Kneeling, Julius began to pray for Ray.

"I was wrong," Connor said.

"Huh. I was about to say the same thing to you," Julius replied.

The two sat on a dressing room bench while Katie leaned against a set of lockers. The confession marked the first time any of them had spoken since the EMTs took Ray to the hospital. The event's sponsors decided it best to reschedule the rest of the matches.

"Actually, Pastor, that's the surprise I wanted to share. See, He never wanted me wrestlin' for the WWE."

"He didn't want you to wrestle?" Katie asked.

"I didn't say that," Connor corrected. "The Lord wanted me to wrestle for … well, me."

"I don't get it," Katie said.

"I do," Julius stated. "That's why I didn't see the glow this time around."

"Huh?" Connor grunted.

"I'm totally lost," Katie admitted.

"When I came to the training facility, I noticed an illumination surround you before you took down your opponents. I never saw how you pinned them, only the end result. God helped you make those moves. Or, rather, trained you to execute them."

"Ray is … was my trainer," Connor said.

"They both were. Ray helped you prepare your body. The Lord worked on the faith side."

Julius now had Katie's and Connor's full attention.

"Look, your body is an outer shell and can be chiseled and strengthened to be incredibly powerful. Thing is, you also need an inner core of strength and faith. Six-pack abs and muscular thighs are just window dressing without it."

"Should I be turned on by this sermon?" Katie asked.

"Connor mentioned I wrestled with myself," Julius said to keep the conversation on track, "and it's true. Yeah, other things enhanced my anxiety. However, my inner core still needed repair. In the end we both wrestled for the faith to believe in His word."

Connor sighed. "Here's the thing, Pastor. I'm not wrestlin' at all anymore."

"Not tonight," Julius corrected.

"No, for good," Connor said. "The thing I didn' tell you before … I knew Ray was gonna have a heart attack this evenin'."

"Holy crap," Katie uttered.

"Jeez, Connor, you don't keep something like that from your Pastor."

"I know," Connor stood, "but the Lord said not to tell anyone in case they talked me out of my true assignment."

"Which is?" Katie asked.

"To take over Ray's trainin' center."

"Of course," Julius responded, finally understanding.

"Again, totally lost," Katie said.

Julius got up and gave Katie a hug. "Just listen to Connor."

"God helped me absorb a lot of wrestlin' stuff really quick-like so I could take over. Ray knew, so he worked extra hours to get me up to speed."

"Ray knew about the heart attack?" Katie asked.

Connor shrugged. "He used steroids for years. Doctor's figured he'd have another heart attack sooner or later. God sent me there for trainin', I told Ray about wrestlin' for the Lord, and he understood what it meant."

"Damned if I do," Katie said.

"Language, Katie," Connor warned.

"You're not coming back to Testament, are you?" Julius asked.

"Boulder's my home now, Pastor," Connor answered. "Oh, I'll visit from time to time, but you're the town's spiritual leader. I'm gonna carry God's word to other places."

Julius stood and looked at Connor. The young and immature man he once knew no longer existed.

"God be with you, Connor." Julius put out his hand.

"He always is, Julius," Connor pushed Julius' hand out of the way and wrapped him in a hug.

And I am also with you, God said to Julius as he returned Connor's embrace.

"Coffee and love are best when they are hot."
German Proverb

Dates versus Dating

"'Come here,'" Ben replied, opening his arms to Darlene. With a broad smile and a waterfall of tears, Darlene entered his embrace. While she squeezed her eyes shut to absorb his love, Ben stared emotionally out into the nothingness.'"

"Well?" Carrie asked after she completed reading her novel. "What did you think?"

"Wow, you hate guys, don't you?"

"First, Julie, it's fiction," Carrie answered. "Second, I don't hate guys."

"There's *always* some truth in fiction," Julie said.

Carrie responded with a snort and an eye roll.

"Oh, like you haven't heard it at all the writing conferences and workshops you've attended."

"Of course I've heard the 'truth in fiction' line before." Carrie gazed down at her tablet. "I just decided to ignore it."

"Yes, because ignoring something always makes the unreal disappear."

Carrie closed her eyes and exhaled in order to prevent a loud and caustic response which would have gotten her kicked out of the coffee shop.

"Don't listen to her, Carrie," said Debbie, Julie's fiancée. "She doesn't know anything about writing."

"Says who?" Julie asked

"Says the woman who has to hide her erotic novels in the closet every time company shows up."

"Tattletale," Julie retorted.

"Would you like to know what I think?"

Carrie opened her eyes to gaze at Gavin sitting across from her.

"No, but I'm pretty sure you're going to tell me anyway."

"What I can't believe … is you used a long introductory prepositional phrase to start a sentence," Gavin said.

"Is that it?"

"And you hate guys."

"You too?" Carrie asked

Gavin shrugged. "Hey, I'm a lemming. What'cha gonna do?"

"I don't hate you, Gavin," Carrie said.

"And how do I really know?"

A soft harrumph came from Carrie while she re-examined the closing paragraph. *It wasn't supposed to go this way.*

Carrie thought her closest friends would praise the first piece of fiction she ever produced and provide assurances she didn't make a terrible mistake quitting her full-time reporter position with the local newspaper. It should have been a moment for combined confidence boost and ego inflation. Now it seemed more like one of her critique group meetings, except not as gentle.

"What about the rest of the story?" she asked in a quieter voice.

"I liked it," Debbie said.

Carrie's confidence rose.

"It's good …," started Gavin.

Carrie's ego began to inflate.

"… except for the immature way you portrayed Darlene. And Ben for that matter."

Her confidence and ego crashed into each other and went down in flames.

"I didn't think about that before," Julie said, "but you're right. Darlene's a whiner."

"And Ben is a heartless bastard," Gavin added.

"You think Darlene's a whiner because she's looking for the right person to start a relationship?" Carrie asked.

"Nah," said Julie. "It's due to the whole dates versus dating crap. She constantly has to know if they're *going on dates* or *dating*. Who cares?"

"Christ, Julie. It's the underlying theme of the whole story." Carrie's cheeks began to flush with anger. "There's a distinct separation between going on a few dates and exclusively dating."

"What Julie meant to say is pretty much everyone knows the difference between the two," Debbie said to dial down the tension.

"No, I meant the whole thing sounds …"

"No. You. Didn't," Debbie mumbled through gritted teeth.

Julie noticed Carrie's straight, thin lips and the glint in her eyes.

"Um, yeah, what Debbie said."

"Do you or Gavin know the difference anymore?" Carrie's voice simmered with impatience. "You've both been in committed relationships for years." She turned toward Julie and Debbie. "Hell, you two are getting married this weekend."

"She's right, you know," Debbie stated.

Julie raised her hands in protest.

"Hey, just because Debbie and I have a loving, monogamous, sexually adventurous relationship doesn't mean I'm unfamiliar with the concept of dates versus dating."

"How sexually adventurous?" Gavin asked.

Debbie and Julie eyed Gavin, who seemed to suddenly find his napkin very interesting.

"Look, I'm not saying it's the worst story I've ever heard," Julie started.

"Gee, that's swell," Carrie said.

"I just think you need to remove the date versus dating stuff as the main theme."

"I delete those elements and the entire novel falls apart."

"And the hating men thing," Gavin added. "Gotta change that."

"Because there aren't men like Ben?" Carrie asked.

"Oh, hell yeah. Tons of them, but it's so stereotypical. You wouldn't find my Jen telling people I'm an emotionless android," Gavin said, referring to his live-in girlfriend.

"*Your* Jen?" Debbie asked.

"Well, not like I own her or anything."

"*Own* her?" Debbie asked.

"Best to shut up now," Carrie said.

"Right," Gavin agreed.

"Carrie, these two are way off," Debbie said. "I think you're right on target in the way you portrayed Ben."

"Thanks, Deb."

"Of course, I've been a lesbian since I could walk, so my opinions of the male sex are somewhat skewed. Still, I can tell you about plenty of women who act the same way."

"Really?" Carrie asked.

"Well, actually, no. I don't hang out with them much anymore."

"My dear friends, I want to thank you for all of the support." Carrie stowed her tablet in its case. "I want to thank you, but I can't. Because you're a group of pinheads."

"Debbie and I are just being honest," Julie responded. "Gavin's a guy – he's the pinhead."

Gavin acknowledged the comment with a toast of his mug.

"Just think about changing it, okay?" Julie asked.

"Or not," Debbie retorted.

"I'm good either way." Gavin concluded. "Just fix the glaring grammar issues."

With a harrumph, snort, and sigh, Carrie left the coffee shop determined to make new friends.

"I'm surprised you came to the wedding. You know, because you disinherited us at the coffee shop."

"I've learned to forgive, Gavin," Carrie smoothed down her bridesmaid dress. "Plus, poking the voodoo dolls I made of you with hot pins helped me resolve my anger issues."

"I wondered why I felt a searing pain in my back," Gavin said.

"It wasn't your back."

"Um, right."

Carrie smiled at Gavin's discomfort.

In truth the anger and disappointment dissipated the moment she left the coffee house. On the one hand, Carrie vehemently disagreed with her friends' initial opinions of the story and wanted to curse their names for all eternity. On the other hand, their points made some sense. Tiny, minuscule, almost atom-sized sense.

Carrie never realized the huge learning curve between writing non-fiction and fiction. An editor for one of her freelance articles could ask for changes when it came to the mechanics of a piece, but they couldn't critique the verified facts. At least the editors she had worked with didn't operate in that fashion. A fiction manuscript offered brand new challenges.

"You ready?"

Carrie refocused her attention when she heard Julie's voice. The person she normally saw in t-shirts and torn jeans looked ravishing.

"Wow!"

"Yeah, I clean up good. Don't I?" asked Julie with a broad smile. "Debbie even tried to get me into a secluded area of the reception hall for a pre-wedding shag."

Gavin ogled Julie.

"Get your mind out of the gutter," Julie commanded.

"But you just put it there," Gavin protested.

"Leave," Julie said.

Gavin kissed Julie on the cheek and headed to his seat with a snigger.

"Oh, change of plans, Carrie. Aaron couldn't make it to the

wedding—kids are sick. Instead I'm pairing you up with my cousin, Scout.

"I'm sorry, did you say Scott?" Carrie asked.

"No, Scout. Like the character in *To Kill a Mockingbird.*"

"But it's not a girl in overalls, right?"

"Right. He's, um, a boy Scout."

"Gosh, you must be really nervous to let that pop out."

"I—" The sounds of a string quartet wafted through the doorway to cut off Julie's retort. "There's my cue. Better get to the back of the line."

"Good luck. I love you."

"Too late," Julie shouted back.

Carrie lined up with the rest of the bridal party. She looked to her right and noticed an empty space where her partner should have been.

"Hey, anyone seen Scout?" she asked the rest of the group.

"I'm here! I'm here!"

Carrie observed a tall and lanky man tuck in his shirt while he rushed to her side. A wave of excitement struck Carrie between the eyes as the man sidled up to her.

"Hi, I'm Scout." The new guy brushed his long hair into place with his fingers. "You must be Carrie."

"Uh—"

"Good to meet you."

"Uh—"

Scout pulled his hair into a ponytail and tied it with a rubber band. Carrie grew entranced by the process.

"Let's go," he said.

"Uh … What?"

"The procession. We're up."

"Oh, yeah." Carrie took his arm and began to walk with a new bounce in her step.

"How did you get the name Scout?" Carrie shouted the question toward her procession partner. They sat at the main table in the reception hall. The low ceiling and volume of multiple conversations made it hard to hear someone sitting six inches away.

"It's not my real name," Scout yelled back. "My real name is Charles."

"Then why Scout?"

"I always went ahead of my family to make sure things were safe. My dad always called me his Advance Scout. Well, it stuck."

"Were you ever a Boy Scout?"

"God, no," Scout answered. "Joining would've prompted my family to launch the ridicule bomb at my head."

Carrie giggled and slapped her hand to her mouth. She couldn't remember the last time she'd giggled.

And when have I ever giggled at something a guy said?

"Champagne getting to you?" Scout asked.

"I haven't drunk any," Carrie said.

"Oh."

She giggled again, shoved a forkful of salad into her mouth to stop it, and started choking. Scout slapped her on the back a few times. A final cough, a few sips of water, and she began to titter once more.

She glanced away from Scout and saw Julie staring from the center of the long table with eyebrows arched near her hairline.

"How ... *ahem* ... how well do you know Julie?" Carrie asked to change the subject.

"We were practically brother and sister growing up," Scout said. "She and I used to play for hours in my parent's yard. We even had a secret hiding spot inside a huge oak tree we used to call our house."

"Like you were married?"

"Like Felix and Oscar. I constantly asked her to clean up her messes. I like a tidy place to live. At least that's what my girlfriend says."

The world around Carrie began to dim.

"I meant ex-girlfriend," Scout corrected. "It's a pretty new breakup, and I'm still getting used to it."

The world around Carrie brightened. *I even hear music coming from the heavens.*

"Want to dance?"

The world came back into focus, and Carrie realized the music came from the band on the opposite side of the hall.

"What did you ask?"

"Do you want to dance?"

"Well, you know, um –"

"Excuse me."

Carrie turned to see Gavin standing behind her chair.

"I wondered if I could take Carrie away from your attention before her dance card gets too full."

"Um, sure," Scout said. He turned to tackle the chicken breast placed in front of him.

Gavin grabbed Carrie's wrist. "Come on, let's cut a rug."

"Cut a rug? Are you from the 1920s?"

"What? Jen likes when I say it," Gavin said.

"All right, F. Scott," Carrie retorted.

Despite her comments, Carrie loved to dance with Gavin. Blessed with natural rhythm, he'd never lacked a dance partner since she first met him in high school. Other folks Carrie partnered with made it feel like she could fall at any moment. Gavin's steps were so smooth she barely had to think where to move her feet.

"So, what about this Scout?"

"Hm?" Carrie asked, lost in the flow of the movements.

"Tall guy, thin, glorious wavy hair which seems to move on its own?"

"You're jealous of the hair, aren't you?"

Gavin removed a hand from Carrie's waist to rub his bald pate. "You're damn right I am!"

"He's nice," Carrie answered. "Haven't gotten to talk to him much yet."

"You were sure giggling a lot."

Carrie blushed. "You heard me from your table?"

"They heard that high-pitched keen at the bandstand, Carrie, which brings me to the conclusion you want to date him."

"I might want to go on a *date* with him, but I'm certainly not thinking of *dating* him. Hell, I don't even know his last name."

Gavin rolled his eyes. "This again? I thought we got past that discussion after you stormed out of the coffee house."

"I got over your grossly unfair critique of my work, and not over the difference between dating and going on a date."

The music swelled, and Gavin swung Carrie around in a wide circle. Other dancing couples oohed at the move.

"Take it easy, Fred."

"No problem, Ginger," Gavin said.

Now facing the head table, Carrie noticed Scout staring in her direction.

"Yeah, I'm going to ask him out," Carrie said.

"You're going to ask *him*?"

"Well, if he doesn't ask me first."

They swung around again, allowing Gavin to glance toward the head table. "Well, considering he's looking at you with sad puppy eyes and ignoring the food on his fork, I'm pretty sure he's going to ask you first. Just be careful."

"Why?"

"Guys with long luxurious hair can be trouble."

"Wait. You used to have long hair."

Gavin smiled and dipped Carrie to the floor. "Exactly."

"'Come here,' Ben replied, opening his arms to Darlene. With a broad smile and a waterfall of tears, Darlene entered his embrace. She squeezed her eyes shut to absorb his love. Ben raised his face to hers, and their lips brushed. Fireworks blossomed inside Darlene's eyelids.'"

"So, this is what happens to your writing after one month, huh?"

"One glorious, magnificent, beautiful month, Julie," Carrie responded.

"Use enough adjectives there?" Gavin asked.

"I'm a writer."

"I stand corrected," Gavin said.

"Julie, why didn't you ever tell me about Scout? Let alone tell me he lived in the city?"

"The man's a chick magnet. Hell, if I was straight and he wasn't my cousin ..."

"TMI! TMI!" said Gavin, hands covering his ears.

"Said the man who probably writes journal entries on his sexual fantasies," Carrie said.

"Hey, I've only written about them for reference purposes," Gavin said.

"In other words, to find the right one for *Penthouse Forum*," Carrie said.

"Exactly."

"The point I'm trying to make," Julie said while staring down Gavin, "is your dating paths never crossed."

"Well, at least you thought of me," Carrie said.

"Yes, I'll go with that answer."

"So, you two officially *dating*?" Gavin asked while he added agave syrup to his tea.

"We're enjoying each other's company," Carrie said.

"Excuse me?"

"I said we're enjoying each other's company. Having a good time."

"Does that mean you're just *going on dates*?" Gavin asked.

"Well, we've been seeing a lot of each other."

"And does that mean you two are dating?"

"Technically—"

Gavin dropped the syrup bottle and raised his hands in frustration. "Christ."

"What?"

"Aren't you the one who threw a fit because we didn't get the definitions of going on dates and dating correct?"

"Yes, but—"

"Oh, no, you don't get out of it that easy."

Gavin got up from his chair and moved over to the sofa where Carrie sat.

"You don't get to add a new definition to the list after you harangued us. You're either *going on dates* or you're *dating*. Which category do you and Scout fall under?"

Carrie leered at Gavin, then turned toward Julie.

"I'm with him," Julie responded.

"I've only gone out with him for a month," Carrie said.

"A glorious, magnificent month," Gavin corrected.

"You forgot beautiful," Julie added.

"You're being jerkoffs again," Carrie said.

"You're on dangerous ground, Carrie," Julie said. "I'm not saying it because he's my cousin, and, if you hurt him, I'll take you down. Scout has a sensitive soul."

"You called him a chick magnet," Carrie said.

"Chick magnets have feelings," Julie responded.

"Hell, take a look at me," Gavin said.

Carrie and Julie gazed Gavin's direction. With an audible gulp, he returned to his seat and resumed the sweetening of his tea.

"Scout has always gotten his feelings hurt," Julie resumed. "He gets smitten by someone who doesn't return the affection, and it's days of him binging on *Breaking Bad* with the curtains drawn. In other words try not to screw this up – for both your sakes."

"Fine. I'll provide an answer if he happens to bring the topic up. Though, to be honest, we're having so much fun together I don't think he really cares."

"So, are we officially dating?"

Carrie spun around so fast at Scout's question that the bowling ball she held flew from her hands. Other bowlers scurried out of the way, and the ball slammed into the upper platform.

"God ..."

With a constant stream of mumbled apologies, Carrie retrieved the ball and sat next to Scout.

"I never realized someone's face could get so red," Scout said with a chuckle.

Carrie poked him playfully in the ribs. "Sorry, I got startled by something."

Scout put an arm around her shoulder. "Hmm, was it the question I just asked you?"

Carrie dropped the ball, making a loud thud on the wood. Nearby bowlers took a step back.

"Did Julie tell you to ask?"

"Haven't talked to her in a few days," Scout admitted. "It's just, well, I want to know where this relationship is going."

Relationship? Carrie thought.

"Advance Scout, remember?"

"What?"

"That's what my parents called me," Scout reminded her. "Right now I'm looking ahead to our future."

Future?

"Sure, we've only known each other for a month or so—"

"A glorious, magnificent, beautiful month," Carrie added.

Scout smiled and brushed a wisp of hair away from her eyes. "Has Julie told you what I said about our time together?"

"Scout—"

He put up a hand to stop her. "I know it isn't the best idea to ask you out of the blue, but I'm interested in knowing what you think."

Thoughts raced around the NASCAR track of her mind. *She* normally asked this type of question after going out with someone for a few months. It was the reason she became so obsessed in the first place with the definitions of going on dates and dating. Guys who said they were dating only meant they were going out occasionally instead of building a relationship. She had never been on the other side of the question, and it baffled her to no end.

"I need some time," she said in a quiet voice.

"Oh?"

The brightness of Scout's features seemed to crumble. Her stomach churned at the mass of stirred up emotions.

"I mean, well, it's so new and all," Carrie looked anywhere but into Scout's eyes, "I'm just not sure how I feel about dating."

"Are you seeing other people?" Scout asked.

"What? No! Of course not. We have something great going on here."

"What *do* we have here?"

Carrie opened her mouth to answer and closed it with a snap.

"During our first date I remember you talking about the dates versus dating thing, and I agreed the definitions needed clarification."

Carrie stared at the floor.

"You backing away from that?"

The question made Carrie scrutinize Scout. His voice seemed tense, but his eyes displayed something between sadness and disappointment.

"No, I'm not." Carrie's words sounded defensive to her ears. She winced at the replay in her head.

"Okay. Um, let's get back to the game. I think it's still your turn."

Scout turned to view the lane. Carrie scooped her ball up and stepped onto the polished hardwood.

You dumbass were the only words Carrie repeatedly thought

about herself when released the ball down the lane and wished she could be one of the pins.

"'Come here,' Darlene replied, opening her arms to the gorgeous and emotional Ben. With a broad smile and a face glistening with tears, he entered her embrace. While he squeezed his eyes shut to absorb her love, Darlene stared emotionlessly out into the nothingness, a quiet and evil chuckle forming on her lips.'"

"No, I'm not too hard on myself," Carrie said after Gavin, Julie, and Debbie heard the end of her story.

"No, I don't think so," Gavin replied.

"Absolutely not," Julie answered.

"You were actually too soft," Debbie stated.

"I mean, Darlene could have chuckled like Satan," Gavin said.

"You're all so full of crap."

The three of them looked at each other then nodded in unison.

Carrie covered her face with her hands and flopped down on Julie's sofa.

"Don't go messin' up my couch cushions," Debbie said.

"I don't care about the damn couch cushions," answered Carrie.

"Want to talk about it?" asked Gavin.

"I've talked about it a dozen times already," Carrie answered.

"Actually, you've cried about it in an unintelligible manner," Julie corrected. "By the way, you owe me three boxes of tissues."

Tears began to well up in Carrie's eyes.

"Crud." Julie headed into the bathroom to grab another tissue box.

"Scout's great," Carrie said in a quavering voice. "Best I've gone out with in long time."

Julie returned, and Carrie pulled out a handful of tissues to dab her eyes.

"He's funny, intelligent, strong, good in bed ..."

"TM—," Gavin began.

"Shut up!" Julie and Debbie snarled at once.

"And that hair, so wavy," Carrie continued.

"Tell us more about the hair," Gavin said.

"Shut. Up." Debbie and Julie growled in unison.

"So why the hell am I so afraid to commit to him?

"Because you want to make sure he's the right one," Julie said.

"Because you're secretly in love with me," Gavin said.

"Because you're an idiot."

Everyone in the room turned toward Debbie with wide eyes. Julie stared at her wife with mouth slightly ajar.

"Is this about messing up the couch cushions?" Carrie asked.

"No. Instead, it has everything to do with your idiocy," Debbie said without malice.

"I believe I need to leave." Gavin stood up.

"Me too," Julie stated.

"Sit," Carrie said in a voice so deep that both of her friends sat down and pulled their knees up into their chests.

"Look, Carrie, you haven't known long like these guys," Debbie waved her arm wide to signify Gavin's and Julie's presence, "but I've seen and heard enough to understand your problem."

"You have, huh?"

"Yes, I have, because I was you. Well, not the whole heterosexual thing. I'm talking about the idiot portion of it all."

"Of course," Carrie said.

Gavin and Julie shivered at the chill in her voice.

"Oh boy, this isn't going to be easy," Debbie said.

"No kidding," mumbled Gavin.

Debbie scooted down the sofa to sit right next to Carrie. Julie audibly gasped as if her partner was about to touch a live python.

"What you're doing with Scout is the same thing I did early on with Julie."

"You did?" Julie asked.

"You don't remember, do you? Oh, boy, did I play mind games

with you! I still thought I needed to date around and sleep with numerous partners. Gavin, if you say anything I swear I'm going to hot glue your mouth shut."

Gavin closed his mouth with a pop.

"On the other hand, Julie knew she wanted a committed relationship with me," Debbie continued, "and she let me know about it on a regular basis, even though I kept telling her I just wanted to go on dates and, like you said, have fun."

Carrie blushed at the use of her own words.

"I didn't want to commit. I never involved myself in a relationship any longer than a month or so before I met Julie, and she was so different that I didn't know what the hell to do."

Debbie eyed Julie and smiled. Julie returned the expression, her eyes glowing.

"I thought it could go on forever that way. And then Julie left for a bit."

"Crap, I forgot all about that," Julie said.

"She never expressed anger at my constant denials, never fought me for an answer. Instead," Debbie paused, sniffed, and wiped a tear from her eye, "she just left my apartment one day, and didn't answer calls or emails. Of course, I got pissed off at what she did to me. In my mind she had zero right to leave without a proper reason.

"The days passed, and the ice cream containers piled up. I started to think about how and why I treated Julie the way I did. I examined all of my other so-called relationships and the reasons they didn't work, and I had an epiphany somewhere between my last container of Chunky Monkey and my next box of Twinkies. You see, I was—"

"Afraid," Carrie said.

Debbie slapped her hands on her thighs.

"Way to ruin my story, Carrie," she said with a grin. "Anyway, once I came to that conclusion, I groveled my way back into Julie's life."

The only sound in the apartment came from the ticking of a wall clock. Carrie's head remained lowered, tears dripping onto her lap.

"Be afraid of snakes, spiders, and a Kardashian coming into your house," Debbie said softly. "But don't get scared of letting someone else into your heart. You have to take that chance at some point and see where it goes."

Carrie heard sniffles and looked up. Both Gavin and Julie reached for tissues to dab at their eyes.

"Softies," Debbie rasped.

Carrie turned her attention back to Debbie. She squeezed Debbie's hand, rose, and walked out of the apartment.

"Well, if there's any positive news that comes out of this," Gavin said, "it's that Carrie is probably more pissed at you than with us."

Carrie sat on the floor near the bank of elevators down the hallway from her friend's apartment, her face pushed against her knees to quiet the sobs that wouldn't stop. She heard the elevator halt a few times during her crying jag but didn't scan the people exiting or their reactions. She was pretty sure they were probably hugging the hallway's opposite wall in an attempt to avoid her.

She really didn't care at this point in her emotional collapse. The anger she first felt at Debbie's statements eventually turned into a mixture of denial, guilt, and self-hatred.

Swell. I'm a great role model for women, she thought. And women writers. Well, maybe not Sylvia Plath.

She noticed the electronic chime of the elevator again and tried to bury her face further into her kneecaps. She heard the door open, footsteps come near, and stop.

"Want some company?"

Carrie glanced up at the sound of the familiar voice.

"Of course," she said. "I'm at my lowest point, feeling like total crap that I screwed up our relationship, and here you come with your good looks and wavy hair and all that."

"Um, okay, I guess," Scout said.

"What the hell, sit down," Carrie said, patting a space next to her. "Come share in the utter despondence of my life."

"As long as you insist."

The first few moments of their impromptu reunion were filled with Carrie's loud sniffles and coughs.

"Sooo," Scout said, "how're you doing?"

"Just dandy," Carrie said, softly banging her head against the wall.

"You probably think I'm mad at you."

"Tiny bit," she said.

"Actually, I'm not," Scout said. "Sure, at first I was upset. I mean, I really like you, and I think we can be great together."

"Go ahead, rub it in," Carrie said.

"I got to thinking about it after I dropped you home after bowling, and I realized I screwed up."

Carrie gazed into Scout's eyes for the first time since he arrived.

"Come again?" she asked.

"I dropped the whole dating thing on you without warning. Hell, it never even came up in discussion over the last month except when talking about your novel, so why should you have been aware of what I thought? Plus, I did it in a public place."

Carrie continued to stare.

"So, you're saying it's your fault?" she asked.

Scout shrugged. "Pretty much, though I'm not the one who left a few dents on the floor dropping the bowling ball. That's pretty much on you."

"Ah," Carrie said. "Well, Mr. Boy Scout, you're not getting off that easy."

Scout now went wide-eyed. "What did I do now?"

"You don't get to pull that chivalrous crap just because you're the guy with the great eyes that all the women fall for. I know it's hard for you to understand, but we females can be at fault for these types of things."

"You're saying it's still your fault?" Scout asked.

"Damn right it is." Carrie reached out and flipped the hair away from Gavin's face. "Your flowing locks getting in the way of hearing things?"

Scout began to smile, then thought better of it when he saw Carrie's scowl.

"That's right, I mucked it up. We saw each other on a regular basis for over a month, and I never even considered that we were an item. No, scratch that. I didn't want to consider that we were an item."

"Why?"

"Because I'm afraid, dammit! I don't want to give my heart to you and have it smashed like all the other times."

"Has it been smashed a lot?" Scout asked.

"Too many times to count," Carrie said, once again tightly hugging her legs.

Scout scanned the hallway, and Carrie sighed.

"Did you happen to talk to Debbie?" Scout asked to break the tension-filled quiet.

"Yes. Why?" Carrie asked.

"Because I told her the exact same thing you just told me when I asked her if I should date you on a regular basis."

Carrie's head snapped up so fast she slammed it against the wall.

"Ow! You mean you talked to her before you talked to me?"

"Well, her and Julie," Scout said.

"And she told you about her own doubts?" Carrie asked.

"Yep."

"And she explained how she drowned her sorrows in sugary snacks?"

"Chunky Monkey and Twinkies, I believe," Scout said.

"Damn," whispered Carrie. "No wonder it sounded rehearsed."

Carrie looked at Scout, who seemed dumbfounded that they both got the same advice. She smiled, giggled, and burst out laughing. For the briefest moment, Scout watched her, but he soon joined Carrie in a laughing fit.

"Why the hell should Carrie be mad at me?" Debbie asked.

"You were mean," Gavin answered.

"I call it being truthful," Debbie countered.

"Same thing."

"In your crazy world," Debbie said.

"Crazy good," Gavin clarified.

Debbie clucked her tongue in annoyance and turned toward Julie.

"How do you remain friends with this douchebag?"

Julie stayed silent as she aimed her attention at the apartment door.

"She ignores me," Gavin said.

"Listen, do you hear something?" Julie asked.

Gavin and Debbie eyed the door. They all got up, opened it, and glanced down the hallway. Carrie and Scout held their sides, peals of laughter bursting from them both.

"Do you think we need to call an ambulance?" Gavin asked.

"Hey!" Julie shouted in Carrie's and Scout's direction.

Both of them stopped laughing, looked at the trio hanging out of the door, and began to laugh harder.

"Let's just walk away and lock the door," Julie led the other two back into the apartment with a roll of her eyes.

"My God, they must think we're insane," Scout said between chuckles.

"I think we're insane," Carrie's giggles subsided.

They both regained their composure and sat back against the wall, breathing hard.

"What now?" Scout asked.

"Now, you put your arm around me," Carrie said. "I put my head on your shoulder, and we sit quietly in order to figure out the 'what' part."

Scout wrapped his arm around Carrie's shoulders, she leaned against him, and they sat quietly staring at the Exit sign at the opposite end of the hallway.

"'Darlene and Ben opened their arms to each other. With broad smiles and tear-glistened faces they absorbed each other's love. Forgetting the whole concept of going on dates or dating, both stared into a glorious future.'"

"Well?" Carrie asked.

"I can't believe you used a past participle to start a sentence," Gavin said.

"Besides the grammar."

"Grammar is the most important thing," Gavin said.

"I think it's great, Carrie," Debbie said, squeezing her shoulder.

"It's okay," Julie said, reaching for her scone.

"Ahem," Debbie said.

"I meant to say it's great, Carrie," Julie corrected herself.

"I love it."

Carrie turned to Scout and gave him a hard kiss on the lips.

"Get a room," Gavin said.

"We're in a room," Scout said.

"I meant a room besides our little coffee shop alcove," Gavin corrected.

"You'd probably have a camera in whatever room we went to," Carrie said.

"I don't do that type of stuff … anymore."

"What's the next move?" Debbie asked.

"Critique group, edit, removal of that whole dates versus dating thing, more edits, then submission. I'm thinking it's a great book for those readers not into zombies, glittery vampires, or dystopian futures."

"So, not expecting a lot of sales, then?" Julie asked

"Julie ..." said Debbie.

"I think it'll do great," Scout said.

"Of course you do," Carrie answered. "You're my boyfriend."

"Whipped!" Gavin coughed into his hand.

"You've made Darlene and Ben a much more likable couple," Julie said. "Resolving the dates versus dating thing worked."

"They didn't resolve it – they just put it on the back burner."

"I don't get it," Julie said.

"They stopped being afraid and decided to let their hearts determine what stage of the relationship they were in," Debbie said.

Carrie gave her a toast with her coffee cup.

"Anyway, I wouldn't mind seeing them in another story," Julie said.

"Yeah, you could add an annoying but lovable male friend to the sequel," Gavin suggested.

"Lovable?" Carrie asked.

"Hey, it's fiction," Gavin said.

Coffee Prompts

"There's a difference between dates and dating."

I pause mid-keystroke at the statement and turn ever so slightly in the direction of the conversation taking place at the table behind me. The young girl who makes the declaration is sniffling, but I can't tell if it's due to crying or a cold. I try to discern a response from the bearded guy who sits across from her, but his voice is so low and soft that I don't hear anything.

Dammit, man, repeat yourself.

I listened to this coffee shop conversation on and off in the midst of working on another story. The girl became increasingly irate. The guy remained stoic. All the time I wondered if this was somewhat wrong of me. Nary one comment on my continuous Facebook posting of events says I'm being voyeuristic. I guess there are different standards when you're a writer.

This particular coffee house has become my favorite writing place. Cozy with good food, I've been a regular visitor, sometimes several days a week. During the earliest visits, I never listened to any other conversations. In fact, I tried to reduce them to mere droning to increase my productivity.

This has recently changed. I seem to pick up snippets of conversations that make my Story Senses tingle. Short stories and essays blossom around just a few words to create new universes for me to explore. And it's not just on the rare occasion. New ideas now erupt from the simplest of statements on almost every visit.

Dates and dating. This one's a keeper.

I open a new Word document on my laptop and type a few sentences related to the topic. I hear no further conversation from the teary girl and the seemingly unloving man. I turn around and notice they're gone.

Creative energy now spent, I pack up for the night and head out of the shop's back entrance to the tiny but convenient parking lot. I catch a glimpse of the girl and guy near one of their cars. She holds on to him for dear life, her head pressed deep into the nape of his neck. He absentmindedly rubs her back while he stares out at nothing in particular.

Got to use that, I think as I get into my car.

"How does someone become a saint?"

There aren't many of us left in the coffee shop's cavernous basement room. Filled to the brim just a few hours prior, most of the study groups and chatty friends have departed, leaving me and a pair of women doing some sort of term paper.

"It has to do with miracles," I answer.

They turn toward me with quizzical looks.

"They have to perform a certain number of miracles in order to be considered for sainthood," I add.

"Oh, thanks," replies the one closest to me. She looks back at her friend, rolls her eyes, and giggles.

There has to be a story in here.

I want my first book to focus on events in and around a fictional coffee shop that not-too-exactly resembles the one I sit in right now. The saint question really doesn't fit into the whole theme, unless I decide to write a story about St. Oregon Chai or St. Chicken Cheese Quesadilla. I type a few sentences to go along with the theme, and save it on my flash drive. It's not a strong idea, and yet a new story begins to percolate.

I look up, and I'm the last one left in the room. My eyes are tired after many hours staring at the laptop's screen, and I feel like they're about to pop out of my head and roll across the uneven slats of the aged hardwood floor. I pack up and head home, visions of saints sermonizing in my head.

I'm angry for a number of reasons. First, I sit in the back room because my favorite is full. This is okay on less busy nights. In fact, I dub the back area God's Corner, because it's where most of the bible study groups meet. I even get a story prompt in this location when I overhear a middle-aged woman tell a younger companion about her parent's strict religious beliefs which permitted dates to be held no further than the curb of her house.

This doesn't happen tonight. I can't concentrate due to the distracting buzz of conversation. The worse culprit is the table in front of me where four microbrewery entrepreneurs argue about their individual responsibilities. It seems one member, the person who spends most of the time away from the brewery, wants to switch jobs and create the new batch flavors. The other male involved in the tense conversation wants him to stay away from the vats.

"I'm going to do what I want to do, and you have no say in the matter," says the one who now wants to mix the batches.

The last part of the sentence sticks with me. I know it can be turned into a story. Unfortunately, their gripe session annoys me to the point I want to pound on their table and tell them their business is going to fail if they don't shut up and put together a decent plan. Twenty minutes into the back-and-forth verbal tussle without a solution I decide to pack it up for the night. I vow to stay away from the back room even if it means I sit in the bathroom.

"I swear, if I don't pass the LSATs, I'm going to be a research person for Crayola."

Oh, this is good.

The conversation between two old friends—well, old in the sense they're college kids who knew each other in high school—is chock full of juicy storylines. She's utterly paranoid she won't make it into law school. In other developments her boyfriend arrived for a date sporting a black eye, and a mutual friend still dabbles in drugs, even after he told her he would stop.

Oh, my Lord, I could write a volume of stories on this one conversation.

This is a first for me. In the past I developed a single story from just one sentence. Now, I have a whole galaxy to play with. Do I create a story with a brawler boyfriend and a coke addict who don't know when to stop? Do I combine all of the elements into one character? Is it a couple or two friends that discuss a potential career at a crayon company?

I nibble on my sandwich, open a new document, and type away, letting characters, objectives, and relationships flow from my fingertips.

The coffee shop is calm tonight. I sit in my favorite room and watch groups conduct quiet and scholarly conversations or watch YouTube videos in an attempt to pretend they're studying. It's cold outside, so I sit near the fireplace.

My manuscript begins to fall into place. I have enough over-heard quotes to produce at least half-a-dozen stories, if not more. I feel a pang of guilt as I develop another tale inspired from a snippet of conversation told over coffee and chicken wraps.

Is this right? Am I invading people's privacy?

Those from whom I've gotten the ideas could certainly read this book once released, recognize their situation, and sue me for slander. Of course, since these stories are inspired from their quotes instead of direct retellings, I don't think they have a leg to stand on. I mean, how can you compare a line of conversation from a microbrewery debate with a zombie/werewolf story?

I dismiss the pang, take a bite of my wrap, and continue my mad creation.

"Excuse me."

My concentration is broken by a young woman who stands across from me.

"Weren't you here a few weeks ago?"

"I'm here a lot," I answer.

"I was sitting over there with my boyfriend and crying about our stupid relationship."

She points to a table in the corner of the room.

"Ah," I say with a smile, "dates versus dating."

"Right." A grin appears on her face. "I thought you overhead."

"Sorry," I say, and I mean it. The twinge of guilt resurfaces. "I'm an author, and ..."

I shrug as an explanation.

"Well, I was pretty loud that night, so they probably heard me everywhere in the cafe."

I nod in acknowledgment and pick up my cup of tea.

"Do you want to hear the whole story?"

I pause in mid sip.

This is new.

"Um, sure, I guess. But, why me?"

"Not sure," she says. "It could be free therapy, or it could be a chance to get that bastard back for what he did."

"So, I guess you broke up, huh?"

"Yup," she replies.

I look at my laptop screen. I've already developed a story based on what I saw that night, and it's pretty good in the opinion of my critique group. Still ...

"Please, sit down," I say.

I push my tea aside, open up a blank document on my laptop, and position my hands over the keyboard.

"Okay, tell me what happened."

She talks and I type. On a secondary wavelength of thought I wonder how I can fit this story in my next anthology.

*"No one can understand the truth,
until he drinks of coffee's frothy goodness."*
Sheik Abd al-Qadir

Without Words

The man and woman sit and stare at each other. Words are not spoken. Actions are not taken. At first glimpse from a stranger, a veil shields two pairs of eyes from any sense of love or connection.

He plays with a keychain on his lap. She reaches for a napkin, blows her nose. He continues to examine the keychain in an attempt to determine its intricate secrets. She plays with the tissue, crumples it up, begins to tear it into miniscule pieces.

A silent signal causes them to glance up at the same time and look no more than a foot in front of them at a young lady. She's in the midst of a conversation about upcoming college classes. She turns to the man and woman. A smile creases her innocent features.

"Can I get you something to drink?" she asks.

They nod. Communication of what they want is beyond the realm of spoken vowels and consonants.

The young girl nods an acknowledgment. "Be right back."

The man and woman smile, return to their hand exercises without seeing each other in the process.

The drinks come. The man whispers something to the woman. She warmly and genuinely stretches her lips to reveal a smile of perfect white teeth. She laughs without sound, rubs her face in something between glee and sleepiness. The man smiles as well. The moment of mirth is quickly broken.

Attention turns toward their steaming beverages. A silence continues to envelop them as sip their drinks, yet a flicker of eye contact is displayed between the man and woman. Drinks finished, the man and woman break out cards. Several hands are dealt. Useless ones are discarded, new ones are picked up.

The man and woman look at each other over the dealt hands. There's now connection. There's now conversation, if only through a muted language built up over years of love, passion, birth, death, success, and challenge. Decades of previous conversations swirl and surround them like a warm, worn, soothing quilt.

The young lady completes her task and readies herself to leave with the man and woman. They put away the cards, clean their table, and rise as one. Eyes now meet with smiles. They clasp hands. They walk out of the coffee shop in a loving and comfortable silence.

www.ingramcontent.com/pod-product-compliance
Lightning Source LLC
Chambersburg PA
CBHW061530050726
47593CB00002B/743